STRANGER AT THE DOOR

Pauline Crompton, a freelance illustrator, finds a unique little cottage in a quiet village, where she can at last settle down to her work undisturbed. Just down the lane, there is nothing but the vast moors stretching for miles and, far away, the prison. However, life turns out not to be so peaceful after all. When an escaped prisoner asks for help, pleading innocence, what is she going to do? Believe in him and help, or have him sent back behind locked doors?

IRIS WEIGH

STRANGER AT THE DOOR

Complete and Unabridged

LINFORD
Leicester

First published in Great Britain in 1980 by
Robert Hale Limited
London

First Linford Edition
published 1998
by arrangement with
Robert Hale Limited
London

Copyright © 1980 by Iris Weigh
All rights reserved

British Library CIP Data

Weigh, Iris
Stranger at the door.—Large print ed.—
Linford romance library
1. Love stories
2. Large type books
I. Title
823.9′14 [F]

ISBN 0–7089–5309–3

Published by
F. A. Thorpe (Publishing) Ltd.
Anstey, Leicestershire

Set by Words & Graphics Ltd.
Anstey, Leicestershire
Printed and bound in Great Britain by
T. J. International Ltd., Padstow, Cornwall

This book is printed on acid-free paper

Especially for
ELEANOR

1

Pauline took to the cottage at once. It was built into the rock they said, and that must be the reason for the steps to the gate, the sloping path and the grey stone walls. It was called simply Lilac Cottage, presumably because of the lilac tree by the gate now beginning to flower. Besides the raised front garden, rose trees predominating, there was a patch of ground at the back that the last owners had kept in good shape, well cultivated. There was a tidy little shed, also, with windows. Jasmine had been allowed to flow over the small porch. It was a lonely spot, the village of Beatlewick almost a mile away, but all that Spring she had been searching for a quiet spot and a home that attracted her.

For four years she had looked after her ailing parents and upon their recent deaths, Mother almost following in Father's footsteps, she had sold the old house and at last was able to buy another home to her liking — and surely this was it! 'Keys to view at Moor Cottage,' the slightly bending sale board proclaimed. That must be the squat little bungalow she had passed in the lane (Thistle Lane) on the way up. She had pondered whether to drive up the narrow lane at first, thinking how long and winding these country back ways could be, then decided to risk it and managed to manoeuvre her little car through quite well after all. Luckily she met no other traffic. If she took this place there was no garage, so the car would have to spend its time on the green below. The cottage had been advertised in the village post-office-newsagent's, or else she would never have thought of driving up this by-way. Still, this was where fascinating homes were found, wasn't it? she thought excitedly.

She left the car on the patch of

ground below the gate and walked back. Moor Cottage looked lonely and quiet, almost deserted, net curtains obscuring the modern windows that had apparently replaced the old latticed ones. The front door as at Lilac Cottage was solid light oak with a brass knocker. She knocked and waited, hoping that there was after all someone at home. To her relief there was the clatter of a bucket being set down and the door opened. A round little woman with a birdlike small face, bright inquisitive eyes, thin nose, stood there waiting for her to speak.

'Could I please look over Lilac Cottage?' asked Pauline.

'Mr Gale isn't at home just now, but I can let you have the keys. I'm Mrs Elton. I tidy up like for Mr Gale.'

'Oh yes, I'd like the keys, please.'

'Are you thinking of buying, then?'

'I think so if I'm satisfied with the rest of it inside.'

'It's a funny cottage. Not my cup of tea at all.'

Pauline smiled. Mrs Elton wasn't a very good saleswoman for whoever owned the cottage up the lane.

'But maybe like the Strettons before you, you'll take to the funny place. Up and down like a gnome's den.'

This part of the world was full of suspicions of mischievous little gnomes, Pauline knew, and no doubt Mrs Elton had been born and bred amongst them.

'If you'll let me have the keys I'll go and see, but I'm sure I'll take to it. I have a feeling about the place.'

The woman turned quickly aside with her birdlike movements, lifted a small bunch of keys off a hook on the wall and gave them to Pauline. 'Take your time, no hurry, but lock up well afterwards, won't you? It's lonely about here. Sometimes gypsies and tramps, and of course the jail back over the moors there.'

'I'll be careful and I won't be long, Mrs Elton.'

'Seems a lonely place for a young woman — that is if you'll be by yourself?' She looked Pauline over curiously.

'I'm used to my own company. I like quiet surroundings, so you needn't worry about that.'

'Well — '

Pauline backed away before the woman could try to fathom out any more of her private life. She seemed the sort of inquisitive little thing who would poke her beak of a nose into everything however well-meaning.

Eagerly Pauline went back to Lilac Cottage, up the steps and path through rockeries and rose-trees to the oak door. She turned the key with ease and entered. Straight into a large bright room with windows to left and right, and a door ahead in front of her that led to the rest of the cottage apparently. This room alone was a delight. The windows on her right looked over the lane down to Moor Cottage, those on the left gave a magnificent view of the expanse of undulating green moors, dark in patches with heather clumps and ferns, yellow spreads of gorse. She went down to the other door and found it locked. There was a key on the bunch that fitted and the door opened, and here was the answer to Mrs Elton's information of a 'funny place.' Stone steps went down to the rest of the abode. Still with a thrill of excitement she went down. The kitchen was here with an electric cooker and next to it a larder hardly bigger than a cupboard, and then the bedroom. Next along the narrow stone passage a tiny room still with discarded cardboard boxes, bits and pieces of the last dwellers, a storeroom. Last of all the bathroom, etcetera, next to a small fridge and the back door opening to that cultivated vegetable garden.

'It's a dream,' murmured Pauline, entranced. She went up to the big living-room and stood a moment admiring it all again. 'I couldn't do better.' She would put her work-table over by the windows looking out to the moors — that meant her practical trestle table, all her drawing papers and paints. She would be all the more eager to get to work. Vanessa had better get a move on and hand her some more material for illustrating. Locking everything up again, she hurried back to Moor Cottage.

'You like it?' gasped Mrs Elton disbelievingly.

'It's just what I want. I delight in anything quite different.'

'Well, I don't know. It's a queer place to my mind. Why anyone wants to build into rock like that — well, that's the reason they give for all that funny shape. Wouldn't do for Mr Gale at all.'

What made her so sure about that? thought Pauline. 'I'll be meeting Mr Gale next time, I expect. I'd better be getting down to the agents now and fix up about the cottage.'

'If you really want it I suppose you'll have to — '

'I'll be seeing you again soon.' Pauline turned to go then paused,

'Mrs Elton, will you have time to do any work for me?'

'Yes, I'd like to.' The woman's sharp little eyes glinted eagerly. 'It's a funny place but I'll do my best, Miss — er — '

Pauline smiled at her. 'Crompton — Mrs Crompton. We'll make arrangements when I move in. Goodbye, Mrs Elton.'

The woman stared after her, no doubt terribly curious. Pauline wondered why she still persisted in being addressed as Mrs, unless it was to ward off any hopeful, persisting males. She always used Pauline Stokes for her work, so why use the Mrs? Marriage with Tony Crompton had been a disaster. There had never been two people more unalike. Divorce was inevitable, most people — except the parents — had expected it. His charm had won her over when they were both too young to judge, but he was so possessive, domineering, too fond of night life, bright young things and gadding about;

restless, never in one place for long. He begrudged Pauline making a career for herself, and also disliked the freelance illustrating work she took up later, ignoring her seriousness, her craving for peace and quietness. She loved her work, illustrating children's books and for book jackets, sometimes advertisements which gave scope for strong lines and bold colours. Perhaps she should never have married.

She shook herself out of her doleful dreaming, and drove along thinking instead about the cute little cottage. The business at the estate agents was soon completed, she could move in immediately if she wished. Her solicitor, Mr Walton, would do all the rest for her. It would be like a new life, she pondered. Another home, a peaceful village miles away from her struggles with her ailing mother and weak irascible father, and the memories of her tempestuous marriage. She had better send word to her sister Teresa's last address. The girl hadn't written for ages, had not shown up even for their parents' deaths and funerals, so heaven knew where she was at the moment. It was through her that things with Tony had really come to a head. Why did she keep thinking of Tony today? She didn't want him back. They had parted in friendly spirit, but it wouldn't work now any more than it had before. In less than a week Pauline shook the dust of the old town off her feet and moved into Lilac Cottage. She had got rid of a lot of old heavy furniture, and her few essential modern belongings were soon installed in the one big room and the bedroom, the chests of breakables and small objects pushed into the store-room for the time being.

'Makes a change, downstairs to bed instead of up,' laughed the younger removal man, drinking tea out of a blue mug Pauline had managed to find.

She laughed with him. 'Yes, doesn't it? It will take a bit of getting used to, I expect.'

'Never seen a place like it before.'

'Neither had I. That's why I liked it.' She had fixed her trestle table along by the windows as she had planned, and was already spreading out her papers, pens and pencils. The settee and two deep armchairs were over by the opposite windows. Her bookcase, the books still unpacked, was against one wall, and at the top end the gate-leg table and dining-chairs. The central heating radiator at the opposite end.

'They made a good job of modernizing this place,' said the young man, still entranced by the cottage. 'Must be quite old really.'

'It all surprised me at first, too,' agreed Pauline.

'Well, I think that's it, Miss,' said the older man, putting down his empty cup. 'We'll be off now.'

She paid them and saw them off the premises, then suddenly felt a bit down and lost, sorry to see them go. They had been a cheerful couple, full of fun and interest. Well, work seemed the best answer to this unexpected gloom. She left the door open, the sun streaming in over the parquet flooring, and went down to unpack the chests. She was lining her pans along a shelf when she heard movements up above.

'Hello, there!' called a man's voice. 'Are you down in the dungeon?'

'Yes, I'll be up in a minute.' She hastily pulled off her grubby apron, glanced in a mirror at her short curly brown hair, then went up the stone steps. A tall, slim man was standing in the front doorway.

'I'm Theo Gale from down the road.'

'Oh yes. Come on in,' said Pauline.

He took a step forward, flicking a cane to either side of him. 'I'd better not, I'm not sure how your furniture is placed yet.'

Pauline looked at him, surprised. Behind him on the step a cream-coloured Labrador dog sat, watching and waiting patiently, with a harness over its shoulders. Mr Gale was a blind man, so this explained some of Mrs Elton's remarks.

‘If you’d like to sit down a minute — ’ Pauline touched his arm gently.

‘I won’t stay. Mrs Elton thought it might be a bit difficult for you just moving in and suggested — would you like to come down and have lunch with me?’

Pauline’s spirits shot up. ‘I’d love to — if you’re sure it’s no bother — ’

‘It’s no bother to Mrs Elton, therefore it’s all right with me.’

‘I’ll just have a wash and brush-up and come over.’

‘Good. Come along, Bonny.’ He put a hand down to the dog’s harness handle, and she watched them both walk carefully down to the gate. Then she moved forward a bit worried about the uneven steps. As though he read her thoughts he said, ‘I’m used to the garden. I used to come over for a chat with Ben Stretton when he lived here.’ He smiled. ‘I never had occasion to visit the dungeon, though, so I keep clear of that.’

Tapping with his stick and the dog

warning him with her gentle movements they went safely down to the road and walked confidently away. What a pity for such a nice-looking man to be blind, thought Pauline, going inside to dust herself up. His light-blue eyes hadn't looked blind and he was immaculately dressed in grey, even to a quietly toning tie, his brown hair trim and brushed with care. After a glance at the disorder below stairs she shrugged it off and locked up, and set off towards Moor Cottage, glad to leave it all behind for a while. It had been a hectic few days with no one to help her. Not even her brother Harold, from his end of the town. Possibly he was still peeved because the old house had been left to her. They had their share of everything else, but Father and Mother had insisted that, as the only child there and for all her nursing and care, she had to have a home. There had only been a rented flat with feckless Tony, and she had returned to her old home when the marriage broke up. Her parents perhaps realised afterwards that they had pushed her into marrying Tony, the son of an old friend of the family, and thought they were really to blame.

Bonny was sitting in the open doorway for all the world as though she was waiting for Pauline. She had a gentle face, a 'smiling' face thought Pauline, with her happy expression and soft brown eyes. She was a beautiful dog and evidently well-trained. She stood up, tail waving a welcome as the other approached.

'Come along in,' called Theodore Gale. 'Bonny will show you the way.'

Being a bungalow type there were no steps or anything to impede a blind person, and she noticed at once how compact the place was, all his furniture and belongings close to each wall, all planned so that he knew where everything was. There was a coloured photograph of an attractive woman on the sideboard, with short black hair and a lovely smile. There was a white cloth on the table and places set for two.

'Do you like music?' he asked, moving over to a record player.

'I do, certainly. I very often work to music.'

'Work?' Carefully he switched on and soft Schubert music stole through the room.

She laughed. 'It's half pleasure to me. Some wouldn't call it work. I sketch and paint — illustrations. I do quite a lot for a small publishing firm, Harmon-Richley, and for a friend who writes children's books.'

'How interesting — especially as I do a bit of writing, too.'

'Do you? That's marvellous.' Pauline's eyes turned to a large portable typewriter that she had vaguely noticed as she came in.

'Mostly articles. Amongst other things I learnt to type when I lost my sight.'

'You have your memories, then, of colours and everything if you haven't always been blind.'

'Yes, I have my memories,' he said, his voice going suddenly cold. Silence fell between them, just the music flowing around them like a lullaby.

'Ah, there you are, Mrs Crompton!' came Mrs Elton's voice from the door. 'I'll bring in lunch now, if you are ready.'

'It's very kind of you, Mrs Elton,' said Pauline. 'It's been quite a day.'

'Thought it would be. I helped a widow lady move two weeks ago and what an upheaval it was! You never saw such a collection of old-fashioned stuff. Sit here, will you? Mr Gale likes the front of the table.'

Pauline took her place with a sigh of relief. 'I believe it's the first time today I've been able to sit and relax.'

'It's one of my days for Mr Gale. We thought you wouldn't get much chance for a meal. I know what it is — oh, you're waiting, Mr Gale. I do gabble on, don't I?'

'You do, Mrs Elton, you do,' he said, his tone teasing and kind. 'This smells good.'

'Just you tuck into it, then. You've

not eaten enough to feed a sparrow so far today.'

They sat in silence for a few minutes, eating and listening to the music. Then he said, 'Mrs Elton called you Mrs Crompton. I understood you were alone — but perhaps that's only temporary?'

'I am alone,' replied Pauline quietly. 'Divorced.'

'I see.' He laid his soup spoon down gently. 'That makes two of us. I'm divorced, too. Valerie had no time for a useless blind man. She tried for a while, we'd been married seven years — but eventually she went off with someone else.'

'Oh, I'm sorry.' She really was sorry, too, his voice was so sad. She glanced again at the photograph.

'Yes, that's her photograph over there,' he said, with his uncanny instinctiveness. 'I still love my wife, Mrs Crompton. Nothing can change that.'

He would take her back, Pauline knew, however unkind or bad she had been. So their circumstances differed — she wouldn't take Tony back at any price. 'Will you call me Pauline, please? You don't mind, do you? I'm not so keen on the Mrs Crompton — not many people use it, and I don't think Harmon-Richley's know it at all.'

'Pauline,' he repeated. 'That's nice and friendly. I hope we'll be friends. I've missed Ben and Lena Stretton. The village folk are most kind but we're a little cut off at this end, a bit lonely.'

'No need to be lonely now,' put in Mrs Elton, coming in with a tray and catching his last words. 'With a nice young lady just up the road.'

'Now, Mrs Elton, don't be saucy,' he said.

'He gets mopey,' she said to Pauline, setting an omelette down in front of her. 'So I hope you'll shake him out of it sometimes.'

Pauline smiled at her not knowing how to reply, but as the door closed he said, 'The trouble with my Mrs Elton, she's known me too long and oversteps her place sometimes. Yet she is so good I can't chastise her.'

'Whatever she is, she's certainly a good cook,' said Pauline. The omelette was filled with something savoury and delicious. The woman used some bold, secretive recipes in her cooking. She was wasted just scrubbing and polishing. Pauline's thoughts returned to their former conversation. 'Why did the Strettons leave?'

'They were unfortunate — lost a lot of money — and Lena was so unpractical, spent money heedlessly, wanted everything, dress, house fittings, the lot. Ben got another job with a house provided. Selling the cottage will have helped them a good deal.'

'A pity they had to leave it, but great for me. They had no children?'

'No. That is, the baby died. I think that was partly the reason for Lena's spending fever. She couldn't care less about anything after that, tried all sorts to blank her mind to her grief.'

'And we think we have our troubles,' sighed Pauline. 'I'm well over mine, thank goodness.'

'I have a daughter,' said Theo quietly. 'Brenda. She's at boarding school and comes home to me in the holidays.'

'Well, that's lovely. She must be a help to you.'

'She saved me from total despair,' he said gently, smiling.

There was a short tap at the door and this time Mrs Elton entered with bowls of fruit and cream.

'That was delicious, Mrs Elton,' Pauline said, as the woman removed their former plates. 'You'll have to teach me some of your cooking tricks.'

'I will that, if it's possible to turn in that queer kitchen arrangement of yours.'

'Mrs Elton, I want her to see Brenda's photo,' said Theo. 'Will you bring it from my bedroom, please?'

The woman nodded to Pauline.

'She's a pretty little girl and sweet with it, too.'

'Little girl!' exclaimed Theo Gale. 'She's growing up now — thirteen, isn't it?'

'Don't know where the time's gone,' muttered the woman, hastening away to get the photograph.

In a few moments Pauline held it in her hands. Another coloured photograph, a feminine copy of Theo. The same blue eyes, perhaps bluer and certainly bright and stronger; long brown hair falling forward over her shoulders and a fringe. She was dressed in school blue shorts and white blouse. Her lips were apart in a wide smile, her expression almost saying, 'Hello, Dad, I love you,' to a man who hadn't seen her for several years. But still, reflected Pauline, in his broken-up life he still possessed this one jewel.

2

Pauline had only been in Lilac Cottage a few weeks when a book and a letter arrived from Harmon-Richley's. They wanted an illustration for the book jacket in rather a hurry . . . 'You'd better read the book first, Miss Stokes, to get some idea for the jacket. I know it's not your usual work, but Mr Folds is ill, and it is getting desperate. We decided not to wait till you called again . . . '

Pauline fingered the book with scant interest. She couldn't stand science-fiction and reading it would be truly hard work. She hadn't the dimmest idea how to start the painting. She was still pondering over it when Vanessa Dorne's snorting little red car came careering up the lane, regardless of any other vehicle or wandering animals. Pauline knew the familiar sounds and was at the door waiting as the woman took the steps with her long strides.

'Vanessa, you'll be the death of some creature if not yourself with that terrible car of yours.'

'I'm pushed for time, girl.' Vanessa followed the other into the long sunny room, looking about her with keen interest. 'Pauline, what a smashing place! However did you find it?'

'You know I'd been searching for weeks and weeks. I'd just about given up hope when I popped into a shop for a magazine and saw this advertised in their window.'

'It's ideal. Just what I want. Peace and quiet away from the mad rush and noise.' Pauline gave a slight smile, watching her stride about the room, examining everything. Vanessa had never married. Her writing was her life, that was all she wanted. In her late thirties, she wasn't bad-looking with fine strong features, but she refused to make the best of herself. Today she wore substantial brogue shoes and a heather-mixture suit, not a glimmer of jewellery and her dark hair swept back as though glued to her head. How she managed to write fascinating children's books with so little experience of them, was a puzzle to Pauline. 'Pauline,' she went on, 'how about me moving in with you? I'm sick to death of those rooms with radios blaring and traffic chasing around all day and most of the night.'

'I'm sorry, no,' said Pauline firmly. Too many hours of Vanessa's forceful character would be too much to bear.

'I'd pay you well. You don't need all the place. It would save us dashing about to each other.'

'No. Besides there is only one bedroom.'

'Only one?' Vanessa stared at her, disbelieving. 'We could fix something up. I'm used to camping around.'

'No, Pauline. It wouldn't work. I'm determined to be disturbed by no one.'

'What if your sister Teresa comes down on you?'

'It would still be no. She has been so unkind to me, now it is my turn to be hard. I don't know where she is, anyway. Now, forget it. What work have you brought me?'

Vanessa shrugged, but gave up the idea immediately. They were always straight and frank with each other. She could see Pauline had no intentions of sharing her cottage with anyone. She pulled out a pile of manuscript from her brief-case. 'It's Mopsie and Muffet again, but you'll have to read through it to get some ideas, of course.'

'I could sketch those two funny little characters blind-fold.' Pauline leafed through some of the neatly typed pages. 'I expect the kiddies are eagerly awaiting more adventures of their favourite little people.'

'They're at the seaside this time. Summer holiday.'

'Should be some scope for pictures there.'

'What on earth's this?' Vanessa picked up Harmon-Richley's book from the table. '*Valex Strikes Again*.'

'Science-fiction. It's not my type of thing. I've no idea how to start. Picture for the jacket.'

'Well,' Vanessa rubbed her chin thoughtfully. 'Draw something airy-fairy, clouds, misty clothes and things. Yes?'

'That doesn't sound right somehow. I've tried to read it but it doesn't seem to make much sense to me.'

'I shouldn't worry too much. Something will come to you. Well, if you won't have me for a lodger I'll be off.'

'Vanessa, what about lunch? Stay and have some with me.'

'Does this solitary place run to lunch? Now you've pressed me, I'll stay. That's great.'

Pauline tossed a red-and-white checked cloth over the gate-leg table, took out cutlery and china from the sideboard, then went down to the kitchen, Vanessa following.

'What a jolly place. I do envy you.

You're mean keeping it all to yourself, Pauline.'

'That was the whole reason for me taking it in the beginning. A quiet place to myself.' Pauline pushed a pan on the stove. 'I've got some fish and there is enough for two.'

'It's a bit lonely, but I know you're not the sort to be scared of anything. Who is your nearest neighbour or isn't there one?'

'If you hadn't been shooting like a rocket up the lane you'd have noticed a bungalow below the bend.'

'You told me to look out for a lilac tree and that is what I did.'

'A blind man lives there with Mrs Elton — that is, she goes in and works for him. He is a very nice man.'

'Is he now!'

'I'm sorry for him. I've seen him once or twice. Nice to have a friendly chat sometimes to break the monotony.'

'Don't be too sorry, my girl. You've already made one drastic mistake — and a blind man, oh dear.'

'He has had a load of trouble and seems still deeply immersed in sorrow. There's no harm in being friendly, good for both of us, but that's it. So don't start making up another of your fairy stories. Leave that to Mopsie and Muffit. Here you are, carry this plate up to the table, will you? Mind, it's pretty hot.'

As they sat over their meal Vanessa continued as though their conversation had not been broken off, 'I've added two more characters to this latest book. Flip and Flop. They meet the others at the seaside, but Flip and Flop will have a book of their own next, I think.' As Pauline waited doubtfully, she explained, 'Flip is tall and thin like a beanpole. Flop is tall, too, but broader with a corporation, idle, likes to loll about, everything too much trouble for him. If there's a chair he'll flop into it.'

'Muffit is lazy, too,' protested Pauline. 'Too much alike.'

'Muffit is clumsy, means well but

fails, not exactly laziness. You can make them different, Pauline. Give Flop long hair, a beard if you like. Muffit is squat, round and curly-headed, you know better than I do.'

'Mopsie is his wife, so I take it that Flip is female, too. It had better be.'

'Yes, of course. You'll make them come alive, Pauline, you always do.'

Pauline went down to get a jam roll for their 'afters', and as she sliced it, she said, 'Why don't you write a stronger book, Vanessa, for older children? After all your travels and escapades.'

The other woman tapped her knife on the table thoughtfully, turning to look over the moors, her grey eyes dreamy. 'Yes, I've been thinking about it.'

'It would be interesting. I'd love to illustrate it.'

'I often think it's funny how you gave up your career for illustrating — this work could have turned out quite a flop. Of course, being married to Tony — '

'Being married to Tony had nothing much to do with it, although I know he wasn't keen on me doing anything, of course.'

'I really thought you were fixed on the police job — '

'I discovered I wasn't really cut out for it,' said Pauline coolly.

'After all that training — you were good, you know you were.'

Eager to change the subject Pauline got up and started to clear the table. She was folding away the cloth when the telephone started ringing.

'Hello,' came a low-toned voice she was already beginning to know. 'Theo Gale here. Are you busy this afternoon? If not, how about a walk? It's a lovely fresh day.'

'Yes, that would suit me fine,' replied Pauline cautiously, aware of Vanessa's sharp ears.

'Are you sure I'm not disturbing you? Bonny loves a run loose up on the moors. You're quite sure?'

'Yes, of course. In about half-an-hour?'

'Fine. We'll be along in half-an-hour, then. 'Bye.'

She put the receiver down and looked at Vanessa. 'I have someone else calling — '

'In half-an-hour. I'd better be moving off, then.' The other woman picked up her jacket and brief-case. 'You'll perhaps give me a ring when the work is finished.'

'All right, Vanessa, though I expect I'll be going down to the publishers, and I'll be able to drop it in for you.'

'Or we can meet midway somewhere, have a meal out. Phone first.'

'All right.'

Vanessa looked back from the doorstep. 'You've got a fascinating little place here. A real writer's den.'

'I feel as though I've been here ages,' said Pauline lightly. 'We belong to each other.' With relief she watched

Vanessa walk away. No one could call them bosom pals, she and the tall, trim woman marching down towards her car. She knew Vanessa wanted her chiefly for her illustrations, her clever portrayal of the childish figures and imaginations. Perhaps it was just as well for it to remain mostly a business arrangement. Vanessa paid her well, and it was through her Harmon-Richley's had seen Pauline's work and taken her up, so it wouldn't have been as easy if they had been really close friends.

As the red car spurted noisily down the lane she hurried inside to get herself ready for her walk. She smiled at herself as she sat before her mirror, trying to tidy her unruly curly brown hair (I'm getting to look like silly little Mopsie, she thought) and powdering her neat little face. Only twenty-eight, not bad, and they still said she was pretty, but she knew her dark-lashed hazel eyes were her best point. Stupid sitting here dolling herself up for a country walk. Theo Gale couldn't see her, but she felt he would know with his acute inner senses if she was an untidy slut. There was a breeze so she pulled a cardigan over her thin dress and went down to the front green to wait for Theo and his dog. Promptly on time they came at a steady pace up the lane. Bonny steered him deftly aside from her parked car.

'I hope I haven't interfered with your work,' Theo said gravely, as she joined them.

'I'm only too glad to get away from it all today. Did I sound cool on the phone? I had someone with me. Brought some work up for me.'

'Well, I did wonder — I was afraid I had interrupted something — '

'I wanted her to go. I was a bit tired of her company.' Vanessa kept on and on so much about her funny little people, it had been an effort at times to change the subject.

'This fresh air will do you good.'

'It is fresh, too,' laughed Pauline, as

the breeze lifted her hair and set her curls dancing.

'I like the moors, it's usually bracing.' As they turned off the lane on to the sloping grasslands, he said quietly, 'Stay, Bonny. Time for your run.' With sure strong fingers he removed the harness and set the dog free. Bonny licked his hands, tail waving with delight, then set off at a scamper.

'How happy she looks,' said Pauline.

'She's a happy creature. It's a grand place here for a dog, too.'

They walked in silence for a while, the path they took, though uphill and down, was short turf and free of holes or tufts, and Theo seemed to know every inch of the way with hardly any need for his stick. Every so often Bonny returned and nosed his hands as though to let him know she was around if he wanted her.

'You are a nice peaceful person to be with,' he said. 'Ben and I used to walk up here a lot. He was keen on nature and used to find and talk about all sorts of insects and plants.'

'You miss Ben, don't you?'

He sighed. 'Yes, it was a blow when he left. The closest friend I have ever had. I'm looking forward to Brenda coming. Only about five or six weeks.'

'*Only*. You sound as though you are counting the days already. Did she come for Easter?'

'Not this time, unfortunately for me. But I know it was a happy experience for her, a school trip to Paris. I don't want her to miss out on things like that.' He stopped and pointed his stick slightly to the right. 'You see that high land some miles ahead of us? On a perfectly clear day you can see the jail from there.'

She shivered. 'I'd rather not see it, such an awful life. It must be a long way from here.' She almost forgot he was blind sometimes the way he talked, so sensibly, so sure of himself.

'Yes, it's a long walk, and we've already come a good way. We'd better be turning back, don't you think? I don't want to tire you.' As they turned Bonny, as though pulled by an invisible string, came bounding back to join them.

'Isn't she lovely,' said Pauline, fondling the dog's velvety cream-coloured head and ears. 'Her name suits her perfectly.'

'Yes, she's a great pal. Life would be a misery without her. Oh, by the way — I forgot — Mrs Elton says she is coming to dust around your place tomorrow.'

'Oh — ' Pauline hesitated, a little dismayed. There seemed small prospect of her own work getting done with Mrs Elton nearby and airing her views.

'Isn't it convenient?'

'Yes, you'd better let her come when she's willing. It's just I have my mind on a book. Do you know anything about science-fiction? I have to do a painting for its jacket.'

'I'm afraid it's not my line at all. I read Braille now, of course, and I'm rather choosy when I fancy a book. Isn't it something to do with planets and rockets — flying saucers etcetera?'

'I still don't feel I know enough to put it into a picture. Mr Folds on the staff usually does science-fiction, horror and crime story jackets, but he is off sick.'

'You're a determined young person. You'll think of something.'

'That is something like what Vanessa said — the friend who called today.'

As they neared the lane again he stopped to replace the harness on Bonny, and said suddenly, 'I don't like you being in such a lonely spot by yourself. You're on the outskirts really, aren't you?'

'I'll be all right. I've got a phone. I'll yell for you if I get scared.'

'I'm going to get you a dog. Bonny has a family out at Minter's place. You really ought to have one, Mrs Elton thinks so, too. You'd like one, wouldn't you?'

'Yes, I would. I always wanted a dog,

but it was too difficult before, looking after Mother and Dad, and so much traffic there, it wasn't advisable.'

'Now you have the chance. You couldn't have a happier place for a dog. I'll get Minter to bring one of his pups up. Bonny has grandchildren now. All her pups and those following on have been splendid dogs, no trouble at all.'

'It would be lovely, I'll look forward to it.'

'You'll perhaps still have to be patient and do a bit of training, though knowing Minter it will be house-trained. I hope it won't get under your feet, you haven't so much room.'

'We'll manage, it will be worth it. I'll call him Rex if it's a he. I always planned one day to have a dog called Rex — don't know why, just something from childhood, I think.' As they came to her gate she said, 'You'd better come in for a cup of tea.'

'Yes, please.'

They went up the steps and into the long room. Theo walked in with confidence, going over to the settee and sitting down. Bonny settled near his feet. He had been to the cottage a few times and now felt sure of his movements, knowing that Pauline's furniture was placed well up against walls and windows after his own style, the centre of the room left bare. If she had forgotten anything such as books or a coffee table she would hastily remove them as soon as he stepped over the doorstep.

'Lovely smell in here,' he said, sniffing at the air. 'Oh, of course, lilac.'

'Yes, the tree is thick with bloom. Your Ben must have taken great care of it.'

'He did of any plant life. He was a second pair of eyes to me. A patient, endearing man. He didn't deserve such bad luck.'

Pauline gave him tea and biscuits, and poured some milky tea into a bowl for Bonny who was a bigger tea-drinker than any of them. 'Theo,' she ventured, 'is there no chance of you seeing again? Can nothing be done?'

'Afraid not. I've had to adjust my life to this. Just one of those things. A disease set in — just like that — ' he clicked the fingers of one hand — 'It struck Valerie all of a heap, too. Life didn't seem the same after that.'

'Yet still — ' She studied his good-looking, clean-shaven face, the blue eyes looking so deceptively clear. How could his wife desert such a man? He was so quiet, courteous, unselfish, neither *did he* deserve such bad luck, even worse than his friend Ben Stretton had suffered.

'You don't know what it was like for Valerie. Life had been so full of adventures and gaiety, travelling about — such a lively girl. We can't blame her, Pauline.'

Pauline thrust back bitter words on

her lips. She could not agree with that. Most people had misfortunes at some time or other to battle with, and she thought Valerie had behaved in a cruel, hard-hearted fashion.

3

Pauline was busy at her work-table when Mrs Elton put in an appearance next day. To Pauline's surprise, in spite of her runaway tongue, she turned out to be very understanding about no interference with anyone's work, after the first few minutes of settling in.

'If there's anything special you'd like me to do just say,' she said, pulling off her unshapely cardigan and grey head-scarf.

'Just carry on in your own way, Mrs Elton, general sweeping and dusting, I'm not fussy.'

'Eh, I know those funny little folk, Mopsie and Muffit, isn't it?' she said with delight, bending over some of the sketches on the table. 'I read the little stories to my grand-children. They love them. Aren't you clever!'

'My friend writes the stories, I do the pictures,' Pauline told her.

'You wait till I tell the kiddies I've seen you doing this. Now I'll get on. I'll go and clean downstairs while you get on with your drawing. I always keep quiet when Mr Gale uses his typing machine. Have you got used to this funny place yet?'

'Yes, and I like it very much.'

'Well, I don't know — ' Mrs Elton shook her head in disbelief. 'Would you like a nice omelette about twelve o'clock? I'll do you one if you like.'

'Oh yes, please, Mrs Elton, for both of us. I hope there's everything you need.'

'I'll manage something, don't you worry.'

The woman went off down the steps and for some time there were no sounds louder than the clink of a bucket and some firm scrubbing, and the chirp of birds outside the open door. Pauline worked in peace, the sunshine streaming into the pleasant room. When at last she stretched her arms and got up for a change, she set the small table ready for the omelette, and soon after her little gilt clock tinkled for noon the lunch appeared. No doubt Mrs Elton had peeped in to see if she was ready, and now came in with the plates on a tray, her face flushed and beaming.

'I didn't know what else you fancied, Mrs Crompton, but the kettle's on and coming up to the boil.'

'For a cup of tea, yes. This looks marvellous,' Pauline said, sitting down to the crisply-topped omelette. 'There's plenty of fresh fruit if I want anything afterwards.' A little later she said, 'I'll be going out for a walk, it's such a lovely day, so you can finish up in here if you want, Mrs Elton.'

'I don't want to drive you out. I'll manage, I'll be quiet.'

'It's all right. I like to walk and think things over, and I must have some exercise and fresh air.'

'That's true. I have to chase Mr Gale

out sometimes, when he sits and sits and broods and poor Bonny longing for fresh air. Well, this room is fairly straight. It won't take me long. I'll be careful of your drawings.'

'I know you'll not upset anything. You are very quick and neat, Mrs Elton. I'm very pleased — and that omelette was delicious.'

'Mr Gale says he is getting you a dog. I'm glad. You shouldn't be here all alone,' Mrs Elton said, as Pauline was about to leave the cottage.

'I'm used to my own company, but a dog will be nice to walk with.'

'He'd better be more than a walker,' said the woman with a sniff.

Pauline laughed and set off towards the moors. There was no one about, the moors stretching for miles and miles, rising here, falling there, broken only by rugged boulders. Differently shaded under the bright sunshine with the colours of newly growing ferns, gorse and heather. It was like another world — she could be the only person in it. No wonder they kept reminding her how lonely it was at this top end of the village. Yet she knew if she wandered far enough she would find streams and clumps of bushes and bird life, little moorland animals, and maybe sheep and wild ponies. The air felt fresh and pure, hardly stirring her hair today. She wondered where Theo Gale was. Probably plodding away in solitude at his typewriter. She had no intentions of getting too involved with him and his work. She was sorry for his sad life yet admired him for his independence and the way he tackled everything, and she knew the only woman he would ever want was his wife. Tony was a weak character compared with him, *he* would never have such guts to carry on in the face of such disaster.

She did not stay out too long. She had to pay Mrs Elton and didn't want the woman to think she was avoiding her. Mrs Elton had evidently finished indoors. She was sweeping the front path, tipping out the weeds with an old knife.

'Oh, Mrs Elton, you mustn't do too much. You'll have backache.'

'My back's used to work.' Mrs Elton smiled. 'Just see if the room will do then I'll be off.'

'It absolutely gleams everywhere,' exclaimed Pauline, as they entered the cottage. 'Mrs Elton, you're a marvel.'

The room indeed smelt of lavender polish, the brass knobs on the sideboard shone bright, and fresh flowers in a vase were reflected in the polished table. Even her pens and pencils were laid in a straight row, but nothing else on the work-table had been moved an inch.

'Just you wait till I see our kids,' the woman said again with a giggle, pulling on her cardigan and nodding towards a sketch. 'They'll be green with envy 'cause I've seen you drawing them.'

'Here, Mrs Elton — ' Pauline pulled

out a picture from the bottom of a bundle of discarded papers. 'Take this to them. I don't want it, I was going to throw it away.'

'Oh, Mrs Crompton — you've no idea . . . ' The other took it reverently. 'They'll be over the moon.' Turning to go she said, 'I'll be up again one day. Just let me know if there's anything you want seeing to before then.'

'I will, thank you. There's only me here so it should keep fairly tidy.'

Mrs Elton smiled again. 'Wait till you get your pup stomping around.' She tossed her little birdlike head. 'This isn't such a bad place really, is it? Once you get used to it.'

'I'm glad you like it.'

'It's compact, easy to clean up, I'll say that for it. Those steps wouldn't do for everybody, though.' Before Pauline could say anything else she had gone. Pauline was to learn that Mrs Elton would always have the last word.

* * *

Two days later Theo Gale came walking up the lane with Bonny and a long string attached to a quite large puppy, almost a carbon copy of his grandmother, except for ears a deeper golden colour and an intriguing gold patch between his eyes. He kept bringing the others to a halt as he investigated every curious object along the way. Pauline had seen them coming and went down the road to meet them.

'Thank heaven we've arrived in one piece,' Theo said. 'This little imp, this Rex of yours, has been tangling us up all the way.'

'Isn't he lovely, though!' Pauline bent over to fondle the strong puppy and was almost bowled over by his enthusiastic lunge and boundless affection. 'It's so good of you, Theo. He's very much like Bonny.'

'In looks, no doubt, but little else. He'll be all right when he gets used to you, though. He's only a few months old.'

'He's gigantic for his age. He won't grow much more, will he?'

'I don't suppose so. A pity he can't be much use to you as a guard yet, but he'll learn. He's got an old collar of Bonny's on just to start with, and here's some food, too, to put him on a day or so.'

'How marvellous. You think of everything, Theo,' she said, taking the parcel he held out. 'Come in for a while, or are you going for a walk?'

'I'll come in for a rest. I don't think Bonny and I can do with any more struggles with this tyke. You'd better shut the door till he knows he belongs here,' he added, as they went indoors. 'You don't want him roaming off across the moors and getting lost.'

The puppy took a great interest in every nook and corner of the cottage, even following Pauline when she went to put the kettle on. When they returned to the upper floor he found a rolled-up sheet of old drawing-paper and started gambolling about with that.

Bonny sat by Theo, watching the young mischievous creature with some sort of wonderment in her soft golden eyes.

'He seems a happy dog, Theo. Making himself at home.'

'I'm sure he'll do well for you, Pauline. You need a bright pup to begin with. He'll turn out intelligent and a good companion.'

Pauline watched the pup anxiously when the others stood up to leave. He gave a little yelp or two when she shut the door behind them, and he stood there looking bewildered. She sank into a low chair. 'Here! Come here, Rex!'

He came at once, charmed by her soft loving tone, no doubt feeling deserted and lonely, and she bent over him, making a great fuss of him, rubbing at his silky, velvety coat. 'You are my dog, Rex, and don't you forget it.'

His exuberant affection spilled over her. She knew herself accepted, he would love her all his life, it would be a life-long adoration. He hadn't been with Theo long enough to pine for them there, and probably his life at Minter's had been just a kennel and a run, sharing with his brothers and sisters, and he would forget them. 'If you're a good dog I'll perhaps take you for a walk this evening.'

To her delight in a day or two he was quite settled down and was no nuisance except for his mischievous pranks. He never wanted her out of his sight, and he was a wonderful companion, his large soft paws padding up and down the steps behind her. When he took the steps by himself two flying leaps took him from bottom to top. He took a great fancy to the back garden that was enclosed by the old rock wall. The gate was always bolted when she was not gardening, so she knew he was safe there.

Pauline made good headway with her sketches for Vanessa's book and drove over to deliver them, Rex sitting upright at her side in the car with all the stillness and interest of a human being.

'Well, Pauline, you've got some sense at last,' said Vanessa, making a fuss of the dog. 'Living in that place all on your own. What a handsome brute! If I lived there I'd have a horde of animals, all that open space and no neighbours to object.'

'You'd soon get weary of them, your writing would claim all your time.'

'Think so?' Vanessa grinned at her. 'Just try me, that's all.'

'If ever I want to sell I'll let you know,' said Pauline quickly.

She got away as soon as she could. Vanessa would do her utmost to get her foot in that cottage. She stopped afterwards to drop the science-fiction book and jacket picture in at Harmon-Richley's, with a note saying she hoped it would do, as it was not her usual line of work. She was running late with it, and in no time they would have been phoning to urge her on, but she wasn't satisfied with her effort. It was a flamboyant picture of swirling clouds and flashes of lightning, and a well-built, evil-looking woman in a tight shift-like dress and a shining band clasping back her flaming red hair. If they were pleased enough with it, she guessed it wouldn't be the last request for something of the same, and she wasn't happy working at it. Mr Harmon wasn't free to see her as she had expected, but they all knew her and a parcel of more work was put into her hands. When she reached home she was relieved to find it was her usual sort of work, and also included some notes from the readers with some suggestions for the jacket designs. She put the parcel down with a sigh of relief — all easy sailing this time.

She had not been expecting to see Mrs Elton for some time yet, so she was surprised when the woman turned up one day without warning. Really this wasn't necessary, thought Pauline, preparing for action, she had planned for a quiet undisturbed day, working on the new jackets. Then she hesitated, the woman seemed unusually flushed and breathless, somewhat 'put out'. 'Mr Gale sent me to tell you — ' she panted.

'What's the matter? Is he ill, Mrs Elton?'

'No, he's as well as ever, but he's worried about you. We're all bothered. He says keep all your doors locked and stay indoors. There's a prisoner escaped from the jail. Haven't you seen your paper — heard the news?'

'No, I've been too busy.' Pauline picked up her newspaper, already slightly tattered as Rex had found it first and unrolled it. There was a picture of a good-looking, harmless-looking man on the front page, and a large headline warning people to look out for him but not to take any chances.

'A murderer and dangerous at that it says,' added Mrs Elton.

'He doesn't look like a murderer,' said Pauline, looking at the attractive face with dark hair falling across his forehead.

'That's nothing to go by. You never can tell, can you? A pity this dog isn't more use.' Mrs Elton nodded towards Rex who was lying placidly in a patch of sunshine, pulling at an old fur slipper Pauline had given him as a plaything.

'At least he's getting his teeth into action.'

'He needs to get them into that chap's pants if the devil comes near here. You're not scared, are you, dear?'

'No, Mrs Elton, I'll be all right. Tell Mr Gale I'll take care.'

'That's right. Keep every door and window locked tight.'

'I'm used to looking after myself, no need to worry. Anyway, he'll make for further than here, get well away, to main roads and railways.'

'You've got some grit, I can see that. It's not often we have anyone getting out of that place — he must be tough to manage it. Well, you have the phone, thank goodness, so phone if you get scared.'

'I will, thank you, Mrs Elton. Put Mr Gale at ease about me.'

'You keep near that phone, and don't go roaming up on the moors till we hear the chap has been caught. Come on now, lock up after me.'

The woman still looked uneasy as she stepped outside the door that Pauline propped open through the warm weather. 'It seems a shame to shut the sunshine out,' said Pauline. 'Especially now Rex knows his home and never wants to leave me.'

'The sunshine won't last. The sky has a funny look,' said the other with her country experience. 'There's a storm coming up.'

Pauline looked towards the moors. They were certainly almost obscured by a heavy, purplish dark cloud, creeping every minute nearer to them. She sighed and bolted the door behind Mrs Elton and against the advancing storm, hearing the first rumblings in the distance. Ten minutes later a flash of lightning tore across the windows and was soon followed by a crash of thunder. The storm raged about them as though trying to blast the sturdy little cottage from its rock. Rex was uneasy, wandering about the long room, making funny little worried noises in his throat. No doubt his first thunderstorm.

Pauline fondled him. 'Lie down, Rex. It's all right, it won't hurt us.' But he refused to settle till the thunder claps ceased, rolling away to the far moors. As rain slashed down against the windows he lay with his head on his paws, grumbling. Thankful for the silence, Pauline went on with her sketching. She had got on well with the last batch of work, and that morning there had been a letter from the publishers with requests for more science-fiction illustrations, and a list also enclosed with details and suggestions . . . 'If you can help us out, Miss Stokes. We are hoping to have Mr Folds back next week . . . '

The rain came down in sheets all that day and all through the night following. It was still lightly drizzling and the skies grey and heavy next morning. The flowers in the garden bent their heads mournfully, weighted down with water, the soil was soggy, leaves dripping, and puddles down the path.

'Well, Rex, doesn't look hopeful for a walk today,' Pauline said, folding back the curtains and gazing out, as the dog waited expectantly by the door. 'Even down the road — it's swimming. You'd better go in the back, but I warn you it's jolly wet.'

They went downstairs and she unfastened the stout back door. He paid his call at his favourite post, then wandered about still seeming uneasy. He padded in and out, grumbling in his throat, as she put the kettle on and some bread in the toaster. Suddenly he discovered he could bark and went on barking, rushing about the garden with unusual vigour.

'Oh, stop it, Rex! That won't stop it raining. You'll have to get used to it, we get plenty of it.' Pauline took out the toast and went to the door. 'Rex, shut up! Bonny doesn't carry on like this.'

He was scratching at the bottom of the shed door and glanced back at her with worried eyes. His barking ceased but he went on muttering. There must be a reason for his disturbance, more than the rain it seemed. No doubt a mouse or a hedgehog, any garden creatures he was not used to. Grabbing his collar she pushed open the shed door. It was dim inside and cluttered with garden tools and plant-pots. Rex suddenly growled, strong white teeth showing.

'Keep the dog away from me,' said a faint voice from the farthest corner. 'I won't harm you. Just let me rest here a few minutes then I'll clear off.'

'Come out, let me see you,' said Pauline, knowing without being told who the stranger was.

'Hold the dog back, then.'

The man crept out, clinging to the

shaky little bench. He was sopping wet and weak on his legs, his clothes thin and plastered to him, his dark hair flat to his head. His face was as grey as his prison uniform and he shivered violently, teeth chattering. He was ill, too ill to do much harm . . . 'Just let me rest a while — ' he begged hoarsely. 'I'll be all right soon, I've ricked my ankle a bit. Went down a hole.'

'You'd better come inside, and while you dry off I'll phone — '

'I'm sorry — no use. You won't be phoning. You'll just have to trust me.'

'What do you mean?'

He came forward awkwardly, hopping on one foot, and hanging on to Rex with an effort she followed him outside the shed. He pointed to the garden door. 'I managed to clamber over that, but if you look outside you'll find a telephone wire hanging loose. I tugged it out.'

'Well, that was a mean thing to do.'

'I couldn't risk it, could I? I was

too done in to go any further. Who's in the house?' He nodded towards the open cottage door.

'No one else for a short time. You've time to come inside and get dry. Don't try anything funny or I'll let the dog have you.' She could feel Rex's tail waving against her legs and would have laughed at any other time, knowing he had taken a fancy to the new-comer and was longing to cover him with warm, welcoming kisses.

'You can trust me, I won't touch you. If I can rest a while, stop this confounded shivering . . . When will your husband be back?' he asked, glancing at the gold band on her finger.

'Not just yet. Now come inside and get warmed up. The sooner you leave the better.'

'I'm not going back to that place — whatever happens.'

Still holding on to Rex she followed the man into the low passage. She thrust open the door of the small spare room that she used for brushes and other household utensils. 'There's a garden bed in there, you'll have to manage with that. See if you can fix it up and I'll bring you blankets.'

He limped in, almost falling on his weakened legs. She could see he was a good-looking, well-made man in spite of his weak and dejected state — it had been a good photo of him in the newspaper. She was perhaps stupid to trust him, a convict — a murderer they said — but she hated prisons and he was too ill to turn on her. She knew herself to be strong and experienced, and gripping the dog's collar had some sort of assurance.

'I'm going to lock you in, but I'll dry your clothes and get you something to eat.'

'Can't eat,' he stammered. 'All right, lock me in, but if you've got any spare old clothes burn these — don't let them take me back. I've got to talk — to tell you — I'm not really bad — I want to tell you . . . '

'You can talk later. There's a car rug over there, take your wet things off and wrap yourself in that. We'll bathe that foot later.'

'I've got to tell you — everything. Please nothing to eat, a hot drink — '

He seemed to be rambling, and it took him all his time to stand. She went away, got some blankets, filled a hot-water bottle and made him a cup of Bovril. Rex, relieved to be free at last, shook himself vigorously then trotted about at her heels. Peeping round the door she saw that the man was already on the narrow bed in the bright rug and almost asleep. His sodden clothes were in a heap by the door.

'Here,' she said, 'drink this.' As he struggled up, his shivers rattling the bed, she threw the blankets over him and pressed the hot bottle close to him.

'Where's — where's the dog?' he gasped.

'Just outside the door, so stay there or else I'll let him in.'

'You needn't worry, I wouldn't hurt you. You're wonderful. I'm not bad — when I tell you — everything — ' He sipped the Bovril. 'Gee, that's good.'

'Here's some cold toast I'd made if you'd like to dip it in.'

'Fine, thanks. You're great. I haven't eaten for — two days, I think.'

'The bathroom's next door. Perhaps a hot bath —'

'Later, please. I can hardly keep awake.'

'All right. I'll leave you for an hour or two.'

'If anyone comes — don't let them take me back — please — give me a chance. You'll understand when I tell you —'

'If you behave you'll get your chance.' She took the cup from him as it tilted forward in his shaking hand. He was already almost asleep. Upstairs in her big room she cuddled Rex to her. 'You lovely big brute,' she said, rubbing his soft ears. 'Bless you for barking.'

4

Not long afterwards Pauline crept down again and peeped around the door of the small room. The man was babbling away in some sort of delirium. 'I won't go back — I didn't do it — I'm not to blame — I've got to find him, he knows. I must talk to you — I can't go back — ' She put a hand on his brow. He was feverishly hot and restless. Exhaustion and exposure. She hoped he wouldn't get worse, and that warmth and food would cure him. If she had to get a doctor it would only upset him more. She locked the door and went back upstairs. She stared out at her car on the green. She supposed it was her duty to drive down and report him being here, give him over to the police. She was a damn fool, no doubt, but she wasn't afraid of him. She couldn't understand why she was sorry for the cold, drenched lame fellow — or why, yes, she trusted and liked him, she couldn't believe he was really a murderer.

'You never can tell — ' Mrs Elton said. All the same, she'd stick to her own judgement, she had promised him a chance. Convict or not, he was ill, had made no attempt to hurt her — he would limp away at once if she wanted him out of her cottage. There was something she liked about his finely chiselled features beneath his dishevelled, unshaven appearance, she felt drawn to him, strangely attracted. He couldn't get far with his weakened ankle. You couldn't kick a man when he was down. A fine policewoman she would have made . . . 'Now, PW Stokes, you can't be soft-hearted in this job,' she could hear her old friend, Inspector Heald, saying . . . Well, she would wait and see what this unfortunate man had to say for himself and judge for herself. As though to help her in her argumentative, undecided mood she saw Theo Gale coming up the road. She went out to meet him.

'Hello, Pauline, how are you?' he said cheerfully. 'Just thought I'd see if you were safe and sound. Did the storm upset you?'

'No, but it wasn't very pleasant, was it? And such a deluge of rain all night. Rex was really disturbed by the storm.'

He laughed. 'We get a few storms so he'll learn in time.'

'I was thinking of coming down to ask you — will you phone through for me and tell them my phone is out of order?'

'Yes, of course. You mustn't be without that, especially with a prisoner on the run.'

'They haven't got him yet, then?'

'I've not heard anything.'

'He must be far away by now,' said Pauline airily. 'I'm surprised you ventured out, it's so damp everywhere.'

'Bonny will avoid the puddles, she likes dry feet, and we won't be going any further than here. There's quite a stream running down the ditch along the road.'

He knew without seeing, he could hear the trickling of water with his keen ears. She would have to be careful, nothing much passed his marvellous hearing. They went into the cottage and Rex made a great fuss of them while she made coffee. There was no sound now in the small room. The man must be in a deep refreshing sleep at last. When she went upstairs with the coffee, she shut the door at the top to blanket any slight sound. All the same, Theo had his head raised in his attitude of listening.

'Is there someone else here, Pauline?'

How acute he was! It was unbelievable. 'Whatever makes you think that?'

He shrugged. 'My mistake. Seemed to be a sort of atmosphere and Bonny is restless. The effect of that violent storm on all of us, I suppose. We're getting as nervy as Mrs Elton. Would you like to come down to lunch today?'

Pauline got up and went over to work-table. 'It's very tempting but I've rather a lot to do, so if you don't mind, Theo, I'd better not. I didn't do much during the storm, as you can guess. Another time — when I've got this load of work off.'

'Of course, I understand. Sounds as though they're keeping you busy.'

'That's how we want it, isn't it? I've got more science-fiction to do, and you know how that worries me.'

'Wish I could help you. But they must have liked your first effort or they wouldn't have asked for more.'

Pauline laughed. 'They're just putting up with me, I think. The one I did turned out terribly crude, outlandish colours in print. They've sent me a copy of the book.'

'I told you you'd manage something. You'll perhaps come down in a few days. I'd like you to look over a travel article of mine. You've been to Italy a few times, haven't you? I'd like to know if my memory has played me false.'

'I'll be pleased to help, Theo. In a few days then I promise to come down.'

'How about Sunday? It's a good day for visiting for most people, isn't it?'

'Very well, Sunday.' Surely in three days she would know how things stood with her stranger. He would be on his way.

Theo held out his empty cup for her to take. 'Well, Bonny, we'd better be on our way and let Pauline work.' At the door he paused, the sunshine warm on his face, the weather making up for its bad lapse. 'You've got this door open wide again. You'd better lock up, Pauline.'

'Don't you think he'll be well away by now?'

'Perhaps, but while there is no news we'd better be cautious for some time yet.'

'You don't think he'd be really dangerous, do you? What could he do — after being shut up in there, no weapons or anything?'

'If he's smart enough to get out I wouldn't give him a chance to do anything. If he's murdered once — '

'I've heard somewhere — he says he's not guilty, they've picked on the wrong man.'

'How many say that! It's up to us to be on our guard, so lock up well. We'll keep an eye on you and I'll get your phone restored.'

'We'll keep an eye on you.' She smiled. You'd never think he was blind the way he talked, the confident way he went down the path. If it were not for Bonny and the harness anyone could be deceived. After a time, a bit puzzled by the quietness down below and Rex sniffing inquisitively at the locked door, she opened it and looked inside. The man lay flat on his back, staring at her, looking calmer and as though his fever had abated.

'Stay, Rex.' She shut the door and went towards the bed. 'How about that bath? A soak might do that ankle good.'

His eyes remained suspiciously on her face. 'Was I dreaming or did I hear someone talking to you — some man? Is your husband back?'

'A friend of mine called in.' As he waited she added, 'You needn't worry, he doesn't know you are here, but he's going to get my phone repaired. So you'd better have that bath now and then something to eat, and lie low when the phone people come — that is, if you want that chance you talked about.'

He twisted himself off the bed, pulling the car rug around him, and stood up, wincing as he tested his weakened foot. 'I'll have to be getting out of your way, but first I want to talk to you — explain why it was necessary for me to break out from that place.' She stiffened as he came closer to her than he had before. 'Why are you doing all this for me?'

'I don't know — but there's something — I can't understand myself.' She met his fascinating blue eyes. 'Just tell me this — the truth — why did you kill that man?'

He did not flinch away from her pentrating gaze. 'But I didn't, I haven't killed anyone. I'm taking the punishment for someone else. That is why I must tell you all about it. That's the truth, Pauline, please believe me. I need someone to believe in me.'

'All right, I'm giving you the benefit of the doubt, aren't I? Now for the bathroom.' She turned to the door then looked back. 'How did you know my name?'

A crooked grin transformed his saddened face. 'It's on the rug, look — ' He picked up a corner and showed a name tape, 'Pauline Stokes.'

'You're pretty smart, aren't you?' she retorted. 'Well, come on and watch your step. The dog's outside.'

'It wouldn't serve my purpose to attack you. I need help.'

All the same she grasped Rex's collar to restrain his eager leap forward. At the bathroom door the man said, 'I need a shave. Can I borrow a razor?' He grinned again. 'I didn't have time to pack anything.'

She hesitated. 'Afraid not. Tony has taken all his things with him. I'll have to go down later and buy you shaving tackle.'

'And toothbrush, please.' He rubbed his hand over his bristly chin. 'You'll have to put up with this scruffy mess, then.'

'Oh, get on with you, what does it matter?' she said sharply, closing the door behind him. She listened till she heard the water running, then went back to his room. She straightened his makeshift bed and then searched amongst the lumber stacked in a corner out of her way. In a box she found old navy overalls of Tony's, a rather tattered polo-necked green jersey, and a shabby brown raincoat he had used for gardening. They would have to do, as she knew there was nothing else in the place of her late husband's. It was a wonder these hadn't been tossed out before now. She laid them on the bed with the stranger's underclothes that she had dried. If he wanted to go then he would have to manage with this poor outfit. Now for some food. She put vegetables on the stove and some chops to cook gently.

Some time later she heard him leave the bathroom and go back into his room, closing the door behind him. Then silence. She waited ten minutes then went down and knocked. 'All right,' he said. 'You can come in, I'm quite respectable.'

She found him dressed in the jersey and overalls and sitting on the bed, his bare feet on the floor. 'I hope the old things will do. I can't give you my husband's clothes. How's the foot?'

'Easier, but not much use yet. I'll go if you want — but I must talk to you first.'

'I've brought some Soap Liniment and bandage. Let me do the foot up. You ought to have had it done in the first place.'

'You think of everything, don't you? I've struck lucky meeting you.' He smiled at her, putting his bad foot up on the bed. 'My, that's cold — !' as the liquid ran over his foot.

'You'll find it will make a difference. I've had a few sprained ankles,' she said, binding the bandage firmly. 'Now make yourself comfortable and I'll bring you something to eat.'

'I'm very much in your debt already, but I promise you' — his blue eyes met hers steadily — 'when I'm through with this — when I've found Bruce — I'll repay you. Listen, let me tell you — '

'After you have eaten you can tell me everything. I'm feeling peckish myself.'

Everything seemed so quiet and ordinary she almost found herself forgetting what he was — as though he were just a guest in her home. What was there about him that fascinated her so much? She was caring for him as though hypnotized — she couldn't help herself. In spite of his danger and troubles he still seemed to find a streak of humour, she guessed he was a pleasant, good-humoured fellow before life went wrong for him. He was almost asleep again when she returned with the tray of food smelling appetizingly. He sat up, rubbing his eyes, his face flushed.

'You shouldn't be waiting on me like this,' he said. 'I've not had treatment like this for — for ages.' She felt drawn to him even more by his gentle manner and courtesy — it *couldn't* be all pretence. 'Why are you staring at me?' he asked, as she still lingered in the room.

'There's something familiar about you. Where have I seen you before? Is it possible?'

He smiled. 'I don't think we've met before, but I've been on television. Does that help at all?'

'Television.' She racked her brains to remember him. 'That must be it. An actor.'

'No, nothing so glamorous.' He smiled again. 'Don't tell me you watch wrestling.'

'Wrestling,' she repeated after him again. 'I used to watch with Tony. He was keen on it. That must be the answer. I didn't take notice of your name in the paper.'

'Dean Jameson.' His mouth turned bitter. 'Dangerous Dean they labelled me in the sports' world. Middle weight. I go in for lightness and speed not blood and thunder stuff.'

Pauline laughed. 'You certainly don't look much like some of those tough brawny types.'

'I am — was — tough all right — but that's all over now. It was only part-time with me, anyway. Most of my time I helped my father to run a smallholding.' He turned to his food and started to eat ravenously.

'I'll be back later and you can tell me the rest. I'd better get on with my dinner, too, before it's all dried up in the oven.' In spite of his friendly talk she locked the door again. After she had eaten she got into the car and drove down to the village to shop,

Rex sitting in his usual place beside her. If Dean wanted to escape he could use the window, but he wasn't likely to try it with his lame foot, leaving his comfort and safety behind. She bought him a razor and soap, toothbrush and paste. There seemed to be several policemen about, unusual for that small place, they rarely saw one, and the shopkeepers were still talking about the escaped prisoner, afraid of a break-in and losing their possessions. Whatever would they think if they knew the man was just beyond their doorsteps? she thought.

'They say he must be around here somewhere yet — that he couldn't have got away, they were on to him so quick,' said one.

When she returned she found him fast asleep again, apparently quite unconcerned about her absence or what she might be up to. She had hardly settled at her work-table when the telephone men turned up. They stared up at the overhead wires then came to the door. 'We'd better test it, missus.'

'No use,' said Pauline. 'It's outside by the window, the wire hanging loose.' She went out and showed them.

'Well, that's a queer caper,' said one. 'Who's yanked that out?'

'Found it like that this morning,' she said. 'I thought the storm must have done it.'

'I suppose — odd all the same.'

'Rotted,' said the other man.

'I think the phone's been here a long time,' agreed Pauline.

'Maybe an animal — ' he suggested.

'I suppose — but still seems odd,' persisted the first man. 'Well, we'll soon fix it for you, missus.'

She turned over papers on her table unable to concentrate on any work, one ear tuned to the men's chatter, wondering meanwhile how her stranger was getting along. True to their word they had the phone repaired in no time, and the man who had spoken first came in to test it.

'That's okay now. Queer thing,' he said, pushing his cap to the back of his head. 'I'd swear someone yanked that wire out.'

'Yes, strange.' Pauline shook her head. 'Would you like a cup of tea,' she offered. 'The kettle is on the boil.'

'If there's one going. Never say no to a cuppa.'

Their thirst quenched they departed, tanned-faced and cheery, still commenting about the oddness of the whole thing. Pauline hoped they would soon find something more interesting to talk about and forget all about this broken wire. She went down to the spare room. He was still lying flat on his back, staring at the window and had no doubt been listening to the sounds around him.

'I suppose you heard the telephone men.' Pauline sat on a box. 'You wanted to tell me something, so all right, talk. I'm ready to listen. Here's a cup of tea to help you along.'

5

Dean Jameson sat up, wincing as he moved his leg. 'Somehow I've got to find a pal of mine,' he began. 'He's the only one who can help me. We were partners in — you know, the tag matches — d'you remember Battling Bruce?'

She shook her head. 'Can't say I'm well up on wrestlers' names. It was only because Tony — '

He jerked his head up. 'Why doesn't your husband come home?'

She met his bright blue eyes steadily. 'He — er — travels. He'll be in any time. I expect him when I see him.'

'I'd better clear off before he shows up. Now then, what happened to me — a chap was killed, stabbed in the street that night. They pounced on me but I didn't do it, honest I didn't, Pauline.' As she waited he went on,

'I was nowhere near at the time. I was with Bruce Dunn at his digs, and if I can find him he'll speak up for me. But from that night he disappeared — heaven knows what happened. He was going up North to another bout. You must have seen him sometimes, something like me and a middle-weight.' He took a sip of tea as though his lips were parched. 'The man who was killed, Vincent, and I had a row that night, he was always niggling at folks. I said things I shouldn't have. So it looked black for me when he was found stabbed to death. No one came forward to help and they must have known at heart — me going for a chap with a knife — right out of character. There's nothing else for me to say, but you see now I must find Bruce to clear me and I can't do that locked up over there. I've simply got to be free, you can see that, can't you, Pauline? You still believe me?'

'Yes, I'm going to believe you and give you the chance. If you had been nasty with me it would have been another story. It's up to you to stay free now, and it won't be easy.'

'I know — I know.' Dean sighed heavily. 'Somehow — Bruce must be somewhere, even if abroad — I must trace him — it means my life. I might as well be dead if not — '

'Why didn't he come forward? Surely he must have heard, surely he cared enough — '

'That's what I can't understand. We were buddies — there must be some reason why he was unable to get to me — maybe he's dead. Oh, God, no, it mustn't be that! I'm done for if so.'

'Don't give up hope, Dean. You've got this far. What do you intend to do from here?'

'I'll try our old digs first. I'll have to risk it, what else can I do?'

'It's an awful risk.'

'Perhaps I'd better let this beard grow after all.' He rubbed his hand again over his stubbly chin. 'I can wear dark glasses. Old Mrs Burley won't recognize me after all this time.'

As she stood up to go, he said, 'Pauline, have you anything I can read to pass the time on, a book or something? Just lying here I think all kinds of things and feel pretty hopeless.'

His story rang true enough, even including television. She trusted him. She studied him thoughtfully for a moment. 'You'd better come upstairs and look in the bookcase.'

His face brightened. 'If you don't mind. I give you my word I'll keep my distance.'

As they went out to the passage, Rex leapt upon Dean and smothered him with excited kisses. He laughed, rubbing the dog's velvet head. 'You call this dog a savage brute?' he said.

She looked back, her face serious. 'All right, he's friendly, but you'll find him different if you dare to touch me.'

'Naturally, but as I've said I'll keep my distance. Eh, what's all this?' he asked, looking towards her trestle table by the windows as they went into the long room.

'My job. Illustrations.'

'Aren't you a clever girl!' He looked down at some of the sketches.

'I believe Tony thought — thinks it's stupid stuff.'

'What's stupid being able to keep kids happy? I've seen a book of these funny little people somewhere.' He picked up a book at the side. 'Oh, science-fiction. Can I borrow this? It'll pass the time on lightly.'

'What do you think of the jacket? It's turned out rather lurid, hasn't it? It's not my line but I was asked to do it.'

He smiled. 'It will stand out on a book-stall, anyway, so that must be a good thing.' He stared at her, holding the book. 'I can't get over you,' he said. 'You've really got guts to take a strange man in like this — and a wrestler at that.'

'I'm not as tame as I look,' she said

coolly. 'I'm something of a judo expert, so don't you chance anything.'

'Are you now!' His eyes opened wide, interested.

'I was going in for the police at one time. Just imagine, me a policewoman.'

'Why not? There are some very charming police women. That explains your nerve and confidence, your capabilities. Why did you change?'

'It's quite a story.' She sat down by her work-table and he leant against the end to listen. 'I turned dead against it, and I'd got this sketching bug and the chance of illustrating these books by Vanessa Dorne. I'd got married and Tony wasn't keen, and then my brother-in-law got into dire trouble and imprisoned, so that wasn't good for me. Your family should be clean, you know. But I hated prison after — after we went to see him.' She shivered. 'Talking to him as through a cage — like an animal, and you never saw such a change. Roddy had been jolly, attractive, popular — he's younger than Tony — yet he's like a shrivelled little man now. I've hated prison ever since. Some can take it, but not Roddy.'

'He's still in, then?'

'Yes, it was life. Even if he gets any release in some years — well, I don't think he'll live to get that. Like his father — the shock killed his father. So you see, I couldn't send you back to that, especially when you kept on about being innocent, that there was someone to clear you.'

After a short silence he said, 'Thanks for telling me. I can understand you much better now, and thanks for your trust in me.' He straightened up, testing his foot gingerly. 'It's good of you to allow me up here. It's a marvellous room — the whole place is interesting.'

'I haven't been here long, but already I'm very fond of it. I can just imagine — ' she halted abruptly, almost biting her tongue after nearly saying 'Tony turning his nose up at it.'

He looked up. 'What were you going to say?'

'Nothing much, just a passing thought . . . I hope you'll find that book of some interest.' She grasped the dog's collar as Dean went towards the doorway. 'Rex, stay. I'm coming to lock you in, Dean.'

He flashed a smile back at her. 'Of course. That is the most respectable thing to do — at least till your husband gets home.'

It had been a strange day and Pauline went to bed early, feeling exhausted, knowing it was more emotional strain than anything else. She slept soundly, only dimly aware of Rex moving about in the early hours and grumbling, from his blanket bed upstairs, and not sure whether she were simply dreaming promptly fell off to sleep again.

She was always a fairly early riser, especially on sunny mornings, so she was soon up and ready to face a new day. All seemed quiet in Dean's little room so he must be sleeping on, and she moved about quietly so as not to disturb him. Rex had a ramble round the back garden while she prepared herself a light breakfast on a tray and carried it upstairs. Breakfast over and Rex lolling by her side the sunshine tempted her over to her work-table and she made progress with Vanessa's new characters, Flip and Flop, meeting up with Mopsie and Muffit at the seaside.

At last she put down her pen and looked at the clock. Quite time her strange guest was having his breakfast. She went down and knocked at his door. No answer. 'Dean, wake up! I'm going to start your breakfast.' Still no reply, so she unlocked the door and peeped inside. There was no one there, Dean had gone. The blankets and rug were folded neatly on the bed. She went over to the window while Rex investigated the bed and blankets with puzzled eyes. The window was closed but unlatched. So Dean, in spite of his weak ankle, had made a get-away during that calm night, and she remembered Rex's uneasiness somewhere in the early hours — he must have heard movements down below. He hadn't barked so he must have sensed it was someone he knew. There was a scrap of paper lying on top of the science-fiction book, on which he had written with a pencil he must have borrowed from her table.

'*Don't think much of this book. If it sells it will all be due to your attractive picture. I'm going tonight, Pauline. I'll try to get through and find Bruce. It's not fair to put on you any longer. I'm deeply grateful. When I've got things straightened out I'll be back. You've been an angel. Dean.*'

So that was that! Dressed in Tony's old gardening clothes he had gone. Even his old convict clothes had gone. He would weigh them down with stones and cast them into a deep pond, so he had told her when she had worried what to do with them. She looked about her — no evidence now of his ever being there for any curious eyes, and she must burn his note that she had screwed up in her hand. She was strangely sorry that he had left so soon. Never had she taken so easily to anyone before, especially a man. You couldn't count Tony, they had practically grown up together, and living together after marriage had proved disastrous. And Theo Gale, she liked him well enough, but this — this was different, unexplainable. She hoped all would go well with Dean and that — as he said — he would be back someday. Well, he had to prove himself yet, but she had never been far wrong with her instincts and judgement of people.

She stared out of the window at the silent back garden. She'd have to go out and bolt the gate there, he hadn't ventured to climb over it this time. 'Good luck, Dean,' she murmured, and locked the window. Leaving the room she shut the door again and locked it, pocketing the key. She'd put the blankets away later, plenty of time for that. Why, it was Sunday tomorrow, she realized, back at her work-table once more. Going down to Theo's would help the day along, it all seemed so blank now with no one to look after. Half-an-hour later she pushed her work aside. Her early enthusiasm for any illustrating had left her.

'Come on, Rex, we'll go for a walk. It's a lovely day.'

They went up on to the moors and Pauline found herself still thinking of Dean Jameson, remembering his awful night hiding somewhere in this vast waste of land, in pain with his foot and drenched to the skin in the unending downpour. She was glad he had managed to get into her place. Today, bathed in warm sunshine, the sky clear bright blue, it was all quite different. Yet it wasn't as solitary as usual, she could see figures moving about in the distance. Police still looking for Dean. Evidently they still thought he was holed up around here somewhere. Even as she topped a rise, Rex exploring some gorse and his nose wrinkling at the prickles, a police officer came towards her.

'I shouldn't go far,' he said. 'Not wise for a woman on her own.'

'I've got my dog with me.'

He looked unconvinced as Rex came up waving his tail amiably, his gentle brown eyes interested. 'Yes. All the same a man on the run from jail might be after money, or assault you just because you are a woman and alone.'

Pauline smiled placatingly. 'I'll be turning back any minute now.'

'Good.' He nodded and moved on. His tone said they had enough trouble on their hands without her making more. She stood on the high hillock and stared ahead, breathing in the fresh sunny air, taking in deep scents of earthy moss and ferns. It was so clear today she could see the distant outline of the grey prison walls. Poor Dean. She wondered how he had managed to break out, but she knew the police would have nothing to say even if she asked. After a while she turned and ambled slowly homewards. She felt reluctant to go in and she could see Rex was in his element chasing imaginery creatures in the bushes, pawing curiously at quickly scuttling insects. To her surprise she found Mrs Elton waiting for her, a bucket and cloths beside her.

'Oh, Mrs Elton, I didn't expect you today.'

'No, well — I can't come on Tuesday like I said. I've to go and see my old aunt in hospital. She's getting on but the poor old girl hasn't anyone else to visit her.'

'I'm sorry you had to wait for me — '

'It's all right. As I couldn't get in I've been doing the windows. Went down to Mr Gale's for a bucket of water.' As they went in the cottage Mrs Elton said, 'I'll just go out the back and finish the windows there.'

'It doesn't really matter about those,

we don't get much dust around here — ' began Pauline, thankful that Dean was no longer down there, but the woman was already down the steps, and a moment later fresh water was running into the bucket.

She was a smart worker and soon afterwards she was back upstairs with the vacuum cleaner. 'I've a new recipe in mind for your lunch if you fancy it,' she said. 'Saw it in one of those coloured magazines.'

'Oh yes, please, Mrs Elton,' returned Pauline eagerly. 'That sounds exciting.'

'I'll get on with it presently, then. I can't get in the little store room, and from the window it looks in a bit of a tip.'

'Yes, it doesn't matter. I've been sorting through some boxes there — besides we can't get in, so stupid — I've mislaid the key.' Uneasily Pauline's hand closed on the key in her pocket.

'A pity that. Needs tidying up, you don't want it in a mess like that.

Looks like a bundle of blankets you have there. too.'

'Yes, I'm thinking of taking them down to the launderette.' Oh, Dean, Pauline thought, the lies I'm having to tell for you! 'The key will turn up. I've put it down somewhere. Luckily I left the vacuum and such things out in the passage.'

'I expect you've been busy with your drawing. No wonder you forget about other things,' said the woman good-humouredly. She went on to talk about the excitement of her grandchildren over the sketches she had taken to them, a lot of her words lost in the hum of the vacuum cleaner. Not long afterwards an appetizing smell came up from below as the new recipe got under way on the cooking stove. When lunch-time came round Pauline almost greedily ate up the tasty concoction of rice and vegetables and spices with a lightly browned crispy top.

'Mrs Elton, you've missed your vocation.'

'My — ?'

'You ought to have gone in for full-time catering. Everything you cook is just perfect and a wonderful surprise. You'd turn fish and chips into something fantastic.'

Mrs Elton's little face beamed. 'I like to see folks enjoy what's on their plates, and it's much more interesting than scrubbing and dusting.'

'Of course it is when you are so clever at it. You make us greedy. You can cook for me any time you like.'

'I'm only too pleased.' On the point of leaving Mrs Elton said, 'They haven't found that man yet. It's a nasty feeling knowing he's prowling around somewhere.'

'I shouldn't worry, Mrs Elton. He'll be well away by now.'

'Don't you believe it. You can't move for police down in the village. They're stopping all cars at the crossroads.' With her usual swift change of subject she said, 'Mr Gale's expecting you tomorrow.'

'Yes, I'll be there, tell him.' Pauline watched her energetic little body go down the steps to the gate, her old cloth hold-all swinging at one side, the bucket at the other. The woman's words had brought her mind back to Dean Jameson. She hoped he had not run into any trouble and that he was still free.

The afternoon was quiet and she got on well with her work. If Vanessa didn't turn up she would have to run down and deliver them on Monday, and call in at Harmon-Richley's at the same time. She kept wondering where Dean was and if he had got something to eat. She stopped sketching, her pen in mid-air. Heavens! as far as she knew he had no money. She had intended helping out, but going off like that in the middle of the night . . . It was odd how he dominated her thoughts all the time. Right from the start he had seemed no stranger, she had been drawn to him from the time he had entered the cottage. He had walked into her life and it seemed would never leave it, in her thoughts at least. Somehow she must see him again — and it was to be sooner than she expected . . .

6

Pauline was almost ready for bed about eleven o'clock that night when she was startled by a knock at the front door. Rex barked. She dragged on her dressing-gown and went upstairs, switching on lights as she went.

'Who's there?' she called.

'Pauline, it's me — Dean,' returned a soft voice through the letterbox. Rex whimpered eagerly. She pushed back the bolts and opened the door, shutting it immediately after he had slid inside.

'Oh, Dean!'

'I couldn't make it, Pauline. The place is swarming with police like a plague of ants, and they've got the dogs out. I got into boggy land, been in a wet ditch most of the day.'

'You've got a thing about dogs, haven't you?' she said, remembering his caution with Rex at first, and smiling now as the dog pushed eagerly against his legs.

'I've a great respect for those dogs over there, I've seen them at work.'

'You've done well to get away from them.'

'Evidently they don't trust the marsh or else they lost the scent with all that water around.'

She looked at his stained clothes. 'You look nearly as bad as when you came before. Take your coat off and I'll get you some supper.'

He spread his soiled hands. 'Wash?'

'Of course. You know where everything is. Luckily I haven't pulled your camp-bed down yet. How is your ankle?'

'Improving.' But he still limped as he went towards the inner door.

'You'll be hungry, I expect.'

'Pauline, I'm famished.' As she followed him down, Rex weaving around them excitedly, he looked back at her with a faint smile. 'I think I'd die without you.'

She smiled and waited till the bathroom door closed, then she unlocked the store-room ready for him, afterwards getting out the chip pan and quickly peeling some potatoes. She was glad he was back. He'd have to go in time, of course, to find that Bruce someone, but she had felt anxious all day, wondering where he was, fearing at any time to hear he had been captured and taken back to that forbidding, horrible place. He would certainly die there if they took him back. He wasn't the type to stand being locked up and watched every minute with no hope of being proved innocent, no career, no future . . . especially as he was innocent, as she firmly believed he was. He would have given himself away somehow, some slip, if he had anything to hide. Dean a murderer, never! Why hadn't that Bruce come forward at any time? Where was he? Such silence could only mean the man was no longer alive, surely? But whatever would Dean do if so? It was strange to worry about him like this, when really she hardly knew him. She found a small piece of fish in the fridge and presently that and the chips were pleasantly browning in the pans.

'Lord, that smells good!' he said, coming out of the bathroom, looking hardly worse for wear, his face rosy with the day's fresh air and his hair tidily smoothed. 'I borrowed your comb, love.'

'You're welcome. Go and sit down, this is nearly ready.'

'I'm sorry, Pauline, at this late hour. You'd have been in bed by now.' He glanced admiringly at her long quilted pink dressing-gown and her fur-topped pink slippers.

'Don't you worry. I've often had a midnight feast myself.'

She sat watching him as he devoured the food with great enjoyment, Rex beside her and leaning up against her legs, his eyes adoring Dean. Dogs were good judges of people, she thought cheerfully, and so if he trusted Dean she couldn't be far wrong herself.

He had just about finished his meal when they both shot up in their chairs at another sharp knock at the front door, setting Rex barking in earnest. Police! thought Pauline wildly, and she could see the same fear in Dean's startled eyes as he went swiftly over to the steps down.

The knock came again. 'Pauline, hurry up!' came a voice from outside. 'It's only me — Teresa.'

'Good heavens, Teresa! Wait a minute,' Pauline called. She took away Dean's plates and cup, saw that he was shut up in his room then opened the front door. 'Whatever are you doing here at this hour? Sit, Rex!' — remembering how her sister hated dogs fussing around her.

'I could say the same to you.' Teresa tossed her head, sniffing the air. 'Late supper, what?'

'I was working late, you know me when I get absorbed. Ready for bed

I felt like a meal. Hadn't had much during the day.'

'You'll have nightmares. Smells good, though. Anything left?' Teresa wandered over to the table.

'I'm not cooking any more tonight, Teresa. I'm ready for bed. You'll find some tea in the pot. There's some cake and biscuits — '

'Ah, crackers!' said Teresa, lifting the lid of an enamelled barrel 'Crackers and cheese and pickles — that'll do fine.'

'Now who's talking about nightmares!' Pauline watched Teresa lavishly buttering cream crackers even before she removed her navy windjammer. She looked from the suitcase just inside the door to her sister again, furiously angry at this late intrusion. Though sisters, only eighteen months between them, Teresa the elder but trying to pretend otherwise they couldn't have looked more unalike. Teresa's hair was very dark, long and wavy, still beautiful in spite of being free and wind-tossed, whereas Pauline's was bright nut-brown and clipped short. Her eyes were hazel with a hint of green, Pauline's a calm blue. Teresa was shorter, looking slimmer than ever in her tight shabby jeans. Though her mouth was sometimes thin and hard with her other sharp features she was undeniably attractive, and didn't she know it! pondered Pauline with dislike. She was one on her own. Their brother Harold was more like Pauline.

'You're not pleased to see me, are you?' said Teresa, gobbling crackers.

'What do you expect? And gone midnight.' Pauline glanced at the suitcase again. 'Where are you staying and what's happened?'

'I'm not staying anywhere yet. Con and I had a blazing row and I walked out — after all I've spent on him! I'm just about broke and had nowhere to go. I'll have to get a job. I phoned Harold and he gave me your address, so here I am.'

Pauline stiffened. 'I can't put you up, Teresa. This place is small and it doesn't run to visitors.' Con must be the latest fellow she had been living with.

'You're as damned hard as ever, Paul. You can't turn me out at this hour.'

'I finished with you some years back, you know that, after you ruined my marriage. I no longer care about you. You can't expect me to take you in after that.'

'Oh, that old story!' Teresa tossed her head. 'You're better off without Tony, you've lost nothing there. Gadabout, spendthrift, a girl only had to wink at him and he'd run astray.'

'Our marriage never had a chance with you around. Tony and I are still friends, anyway, so you can stop calling him, and now finish your supper and leave me alone.'

'Paul, I'm exhausted. I can't walk another step. Let me stay.'

'How did you get here?'

'How d'you suppose?' The other laughed. 'A chap drove me up most of the way from the station. You don't know how to do it.'

The station was three to four miles away, and the hourly bus finished at 7.0 pm. 'You'll find yourself in trouble one of these days.'

'Trouble and I are companions. Guess Con would have murdered me if I'd stayed after today.' The green-flecked eyes watched Pauline appealingly. 'Let me stay, Paul.'

'I've only one bedroom and a single bed. It's impossible.'

Teresa glanced at the settee. 'I'll make do with that. Anything rather than go out tonight. It's so quiet and desolate — '

'All right — just for tonight. Tomorrow morning I'll run you down to the village. You can find rooms there and then set about getting a job. You must go and call on Mr Walton the solicitor, too, and he'll let you have your share from Mother and Dad. They left me the house, you know.'

'But Pauline — '

'You're not stopping here, Teresa. I've a load of work to do and I can't do it with you around. I took this place for its smallness and quietness, and that's how it is going to stay. Just for tonight the settee. I'll go down and get you some blankets.' Pauline hurried to the door while her sister was still engrossed in food. Downstairs she locked Dean's door, took away the key and in her own room scribbled a note of explanation that she pushed under his door a few moments later. She was gathering together an eiderdown and blankets when Teresa appeared at the head of the steps.

'What a queer place! What's down there?'

'All mod cons. You'd better come down for a wash before bed, and hurry, too. I'm tired out.'

Taking her time, Teresa nosed into every corner. 'Well, I suppose it has all you need, although so odd and squashed together.' She tried Dean's door. 'What's in here?'

'Only a broom cupboard. Probably the cleaning woman has the key.'

Teresa laughed. 'Is she afraid of someone pinching some old brushes and things?'

Uneasy at all the lies she was having to think up (but no one was going to trap Dean if she could help it!) Pauline ignored this last scornful remark and went upstairs with the bedding, from the top urging her sister to hurry up. 'I don't want to be late getting up in the morning,' she said, when Teresa returned, having dropped off her jeans and heavy jumper and looking quite lively despite the late hour. 'I'm going out to lunch tomorrow, and I have to get you in your digs first.'

'I can wait here for you. It's Sunday and you'll change your mind in the morning.'

'I know who'll put you up, Sunday makes no difference. I don't want you here, Teresa, so no more arguments. I can't work with anyone around.'

'You're making me pay for Tony all

right, aren't you?'

Pauline felt cold inside and unhappy. She bade her good night and went away, firmly closing the door behind her. 'Take the dog with you,' Teresa called after her. With a sigh Pauline looked inside the room again. Rex was standing an arm's length away, his head on one side, his eyes miserable and appealing. He knew where he wasn't wanted all right.

'All right, come on, Rex.' He leapt down past her and she closed the door once more. The dog pattered about her room undecidedly for a few minutes, then as she lay down in bed made up his mind that the woolly rug beside her looked the most comfortable and curled up there with a sigh of contentment. She put down a hand to stroke his silky head. 'This is getting you into bad habits, Rex old boy, so don't expect it to last.'

She was a good while getting off to sleep. If Teresa hadn't been her sister she would have said she hated her. She had finished bending to the will of that selfish, grabbing, hard little creature. Teresa was older than she was, she must pull herself together and make her own life. She was not responsible for Teresa, just because she was making a success of her life alone.

After a restless sleep of a few hours she was up quite early. She crept up to peep in the top room and, as she had expected, Teresa was rolled in blankets like a mummy and still sound asleep. She went off at once into Dean's room. He was awake and lay there smiling at her.

'She's still asleep so take your chance of the bathroom,' murmured Pauline. 'Keep quiet and for heaven's sake be quick — don't bother shaving. I'm hoping to get rid of her this morning.'

He nodded and slid off the narrow bed, the rug tucked around his naked limbs. While he was in the bathroom she hurriedly set a tray for him with cereal, milk and sugar, bread, butter and marmalade, and left it ready in his room for him. When he returned she locked him in again and set about breakfast for herself and Teresa, moving about and talking to Rex who was eager now to see all that was going on. No need to keep quiet now. Her life was getting most involved. She must insist on Teresa leaving today however much charm or persuasion she tried to turn on. The table set, toast and tea made, Pauline shook Teresa's shoulder.

'Come on, breakfast! Time you were up.'

Before she could stop him Rex had joined in and was licking Teresa's face. 'Oh, you horrible old thing!' Teresa sat up and wiped her face on a blanket. 'Keep the animal away, will you, Paul? I can never understand how you people put up with sloppy dogs.'

'He's only trying to make friends. He's a wonderful companion, more faithful than most people. Lie down, Rex, good boy. Come along, Teresa, wrap a blanket round you and come for breakfast.'

'Who wants a blanket? It's sunny and warm.'

Pauline looked with vexation at the sylph-like figure in brief bra and panties. 'I have folks calling quite often, and here you are like this and the room in a fearful mess.'

'Who's going to call here, for lord's sake!' Teresa's firm little teeth bit into toast.

'One never knows, they are friendly in this small place. Mrs Elton who cleans, or my nearest neighbour — maybe Vanessa and — and others — '

'Never mind, I'll scarper down into the dungeon if anyone comes.'

Pauline shuddered. 'Don't say that!' It had been funny coming from Theo Gale, but there was no fun in Teresa.

'Why not? You *are* touchy. Can't say the years have made you any sweeter.'

Annoyed, Pauline was no longer hungry. She pushed her plate aside and got up to fold the bed-clothes. While Teresa dressed she spent the time preparing potatoes and carrots.

Dean could either cook them for himself while she was down at Moor Cottage, or she'd cook for him later in the day.

'Thought you were going out to lunch,' said Teresa, coming up behind her, drawing a comb through the thick long hair of which she was so proud.

'So I am.' Pauline drew off her rubber gloves. 'Habit, I suppose. They'll come in for tomorrow, save time. I'll be busy. I'm really waiting for you. I'm ready for off if you are.'

'You haven't changed your mind? I'll be good, Paul, I promise.' Teresa put on her girlish, most appealing look of the long-lashed eyes, her dark hair falling forward and framing her piquant face.

'Come along, Teresa, we're going. You needn't try your softening looks on me, I know you. We never got on together.'

'What Mum and Dad would say — '

'They wouldn't blame me. But they'd have plenty to say to you, though, after your callous treatment of them — all that time with never a word.'

Teresa shrugged and went up the steps. 'It's perhaps as well I'm going. You've done nothing but preach since I got here.'

Pauline followed her. 'Don't forget to call on Mr Walton for your money.'

'You dropped pretty, didn't you, getting the whole house?' sneered Teresa, thrusting her arms into her wind-jammer.

Pauline ignored this. She had nursed their parents through their long illnesses, and she knew they doted on her because she was the youngest, and they had been distressed at her broken marriage and the hard knocks she had experienced. They had blanked their minds to Teresa who had disappeared out of their lives so long ago. Harold kept in touch with them infrequently, but he had made a success of his business and was well-off. Teresa showed no gratitude for this information of money that had been left to her.

She had wandered over to Pauline's work-table. 'So the Vanessa woman comes here, does she? Are you still drawing this tripe?' She flicked a finger at one of the illustrations.

'That and other things. They're fun to do. Vanessa and I are on to a good thing so why drop it?'

'Oh well, if that's all you want of life — the dog's out — ' Teresa exclaimed, as she opened the door and Rex skipped past her into the sunshine.

Pauline smiled. 'He always comes with me, and I'm afraid he's used to the front seat of the car.'

'Well, he can have it. Save him blowing down my neck, anyway.'

Teresa opened a back door of the car and climbed in and Pauline put her suitcase down beside her. Rex jumped into his accustomed place and they set off quietly down the road. Theo was in his front garden, a few tulips in his hand. Pauline slowed down, she knew he had heard the car and was listening.

'Good morning, Theo. Just going down to the village,' she called. 'I'll be seeing you later.'

'Hello, good morning, Pauline,' he returned, with a smile. 'Don't be late, we're expecting you.'

'Oh-ho!' said Teresa, as the car moved on. 'Theo and Pauline. Your nearest neighbour, eh? No wonder you wanted me out of the way.'

'It's nothing like that, so you can shut up.'

'You might have introduced me.'

'He is something of a recluse, he wouldn't have been interested in you.' Teresa had not known he was blind, and she certainly was not going to inform her.

'It doesn't seem to have stopped you getting your foot in, anyway. Lunch, eh?'

'Yes, lunch.' Pauline's lips drew into a bitter line. Teresa would spoil this new acquaintance if she could.

There was a bus standing in the little square as they approached the village.

Teresa bent forward. 'Put me down here, Pauline. I'm not going to any old digs. I'll get on that bus wherever it's going.'

'It won't be going for a while, I expect.'

'Never mind, I'll be on it.'

The car stopped. 'What about money, Teresa? Do you need any?'

'Oh, I've enough to see me through a day or two, and I'll be calling on old Walton for my cheque. I'm not going to knuckle under to you — ever.'

'You'll let me know your address when you settle?'

Teresa and her suitcase were out of the car. She looked back with a defiant expression. 'Maybe. Does it matter? What do you care?'

She flounced away and Pauline watched her climb up into the bus and get a seat by a far window, almost out of sight. How odd it was, thought Pauline, that she was more concerned for Dean Jameson's well-being than for her errant sister's. She had no pity for her, only thankful to see her go. She knew from experience that whatever she did for Teresa would only be flung back in her face when her sister had used her for just as long as she wanted. She also knew Teresa wouldn't be alone for long, another man would come along . . . She turned the car and drove steadily back to Thistle Lane.

7

Theo Gale was no longer in his garden. At the top of the lane the lovely moors stretched as far as the eye could see, fresh summer green, not a soul in sight. Pauline went into her cottage and down at once to unlock Dean's door.

'You must feel like a prisoner again,' she laughed. 'I'm sorry.'

'Not to worry. It was decent of you to go to so much trouble. How you two sisters love each other!'

He must have heard a few things as Teresa dawdled about behind her as she worked in the kitchen quarters. 'That was all killed — dead — some time ago. Teresa will grab all but give nothing in return.' She picked up the breakfast tray. 'The place is all yours now, Dean, so do as you like. I'm going down the road to lunch. I promised so I'll have to go, but what about your lunch?'

'Oh, just a snack. I can get an egg or something.'

'All right. I'll cook you a meal later in the day.'

As he followed her into the passage, he said, 'You know what I'd like most of all this minute? A bath. Is it possible, Pauline?'

'Of course. Luckily I always have hot water, no problems there.' She opened a cupboard, took out a large bath towel and tossed it to him. 'Go and enjoy yourself. You ought to have had this before after that wet ditch — if Teresa hadn't dished things up. It's a wonder you haven't a streaming cold.'

'I'm a hardy piece of goods — we practise hard, the wrestlers, you know. Take more than that to lay me out.'

She smiled. He seemed to have forgotten his shivers and fever of the first night. Still, he had thrown that off, too. He had a good constitution at the bottom of it all. He must have kept up his exercises in some way, although confined within those prison walls. He was a well-made man, with a clear healthy skin, the tight undervest displaying his chest and muscles.

Before she left she showed him the larder and told him to help himself to anything he fancied. 'And for goodness sake hide yourself if you hear anyone around.'

He gave his cheeky grin. 'That's one thing you can be sure of. I won't run off this time. I'll be waiting here for you, love, so go off and have a good time.'

She smiled again, flushing. What *was* this thing between them? They were behaving like a happily married couple! He a stranger — an unknown — she must be mad! She walked with Rex down to Moor Cottage. A pity she couldn't confide in Theo. No doubt Dean was wrong to run and hide, and she was even more in the wrong concealing him, but how else could he get this one vital chance to prove his innocence. Somehow his friend must be found.

'Haven't you been feeling well, Pauline?' asked Theo, as they sat over Mrs Elton's excellent lunch.

'No, whatever makes you think that?'

'Mrs Elton thought you seemed a bit off-colour — her words — or that you were worried about something, also you'd lost a key . . . '

Pauline sighed inwardly. Mrs Elton didn't miss much. 'It wasn't an important key, and I was only a bit tired, I expect. I sit over the sketching too long, too late at night. And then, another thing, my sister turned up out of the blue. She's not a welcome visitor, I'm afraid.' What matter if she mixed the days up? Another small lie wouldn't make much difference.

'Ah. Is she staying with you?'

'No, I packed her off. There's no love between us.'

'But your sister, that sounds a bit cruel, not like you, Pauline.' His blue eyes were on her face, almost as though he could see her. It was most disconcerting.

'We are better apart, the fur flies between us. It's rather a long story, Theo. Someday I'll tell you — but today I'm not in the mood.'

'You know your own business best,' said Theo quickly. 'I didn't mean to pry.'

'I'm a bit restless, unable to concentrate. Maybe it's the warmer weather.'

'Yes, it's gone a bit close. I hope it doesn't mean another storm, and I hope you're not too restless to look over that article of mine.'

'Of course not, Theo. I'll be interested and it will be a change of subject for me.'

'It's only rough yet, of course, but if you have any suggestions, criticisms, I'd be pleased.'

While Mrs Elton splashed about in the kitchen with the pots and pans before leaving, Theo got out his painstakingly typed papers and Pauline started to read them. Rough the article might be but it held her interest. She read right through without a word. It was different from so many travel articles, humorous and down to earth. He waited patiently, pulling contentedly at Bonny's ears as she sat beside him. Rex, who apparently was fond of him, too, lay across his foot.

As she looked up at last saying she liked it, he said, 'It's rather long, but that is what this magazine seems to want, something with some body in it.'

'Theo, it's great. I don't see that I'm experienced enough to try to improve it. You seem to have got into the minds of the people on those distant farms, their habits, likes and dislikes, all of it.'

'I have lived with them, Pauline — that is, Valerie and I. We didn't care for hotels and the usual tourist places. We found villages with quiet *pensions*, more often farms, we even had a caravan sometimes. Such friendly, easy-going people. A bit lazy, but loving a musical evening, frolics, jolly gatherings — we learnt a lot about them. You read there of the high jinks of a wedding feast all out in the open, dancing afterwards in a field, the cows looking on and taking it all as a natural occurrence.'

'I can see it all through your eyes. Theo — oh, sorry — ' she forgot so often that those eyes resting on her were sightless.

'Don't be embarrassed, dear girl. I *had* my eyes then, of course. I'm so glad it rings true to you and holds your interest.'

'Would you like me to type it for you, Theo? I have a large portable. I don't want to interfere but if it would help — '

'Would you, Pauline?' His voice was warm, eager. 'It would be a great help. I'm a slow plodder on the machine. They make allowances for me, any slips, but still — if you would — and I can get on with another article while I'm in the mood. It's going to be a series, you see, and it seems my delving into countries abroad is going to pay off.'

'I'll take it with me, then, and let you have it back as soon as I can. My friend is an authoress so I know a bit about it all.'

'Thank you so much, but don't let it hold your work up, Pauline. I didn't ask you to read it, expecting all this — '

'I know, but I'm really interested. I'll enjoy going through it again. Just tell me anything you want doing before I start to type it. You have some photos to send with it, I hope.'

'Oh yes. I'll show you while we're on about it.' Theo got up and opened a drawer in the desk against the wall. His hand went at once to a thick wallet of photographs. He must take the greatest care of everything he laid aside, thought Pauline, knowing where they were if he needed them. 'I'm sending the five top ones, Pauline, but you'd better check for me. We wrote on the back of each one — at the time.' As she turned over the splendid black-and-white photographs, he said musingly, 'I always had a feeling I would use them in some way one day.'

As usual, when in Theo Gale's company with his conversation and knowledge of so many things, and in the background some of his favourite music playing softly, the time flew by. The cottage was quiet and peaceful, Mrs Elton having long since gone off home. Pauline was making tea for them and bringing in the fruit and cakes left on a tray ready, when she thought of Dean. Quite time she was getting back to him, although she had no fear of him running off again or of anyone finding him there. Theo had never mentioned him this time, so probably he and the villagers, too, were deciding Dean was well away by now and that they were quite safe. It would soon be just a nine days' wonder, and then perhaps the way would be clear for him.

As soon as she could decently

withdraw after Theo's hospitality, she took up his typed article, woke Rex from his twitching dreams and went home. All was quiet as she entered her cottage, the long room tidy and uninhabited.

'Dean!' she called, a little uneasily.

'Okay, Pauline, I'm down here.' He came up the steps in one or two leaps as Rex would. He looked clean and fresh in spite of the shabby clothes he had to wear, his dark hair still standing on end, rather curly and unruly after the bath he must have had. 'I thought it wiser to stay below after — well, someone came, you see. I heard the car and vanished below. They knocked for ages and tried the gate into the back, probably looked through the windows up here, and at last thrust a packet through the letter-box and went away.' He pointed to a bulky packet on her work-table. 'I had a job getting the parcel out afterwards, jammed tight.'

Pauline recognized the packet. 'Oh, Vanessa. She'd expect me to be at home on Sunday. She ought to have phoned.' She laughed. 'You'd have good warning with her car all right. She drives like a demon. It's the noisiest car on earth.'

'I'll say! I thought an army of tanks were coming after me.'

'I'll get some dinner on for you — that is if you haven't cooked anything.'

'I didn't want to meddle too much. I found an egg and fruit so I'm all right.'

'That means dinner for you now, then,' said Pauline, going towards the steps down.

After he had eaten the meal she set out for him, they sat on in the dusky room, the sky a painter's delight of gold and red where the sun had gone down. It gave a russet tinge to Pauline's short curly hair and glowed on her creamy complexion, and he sat admiring her thoughtfully.

'Pauline,' he began suddenly, 'why don't you tell me the truth? You know all about me, now it's your turn. This so-called husband of yours — there's no evidence of a man about the place. These clothes you gave me could be throw-outs, just anybody's. There is no husband, is there?' As she hesitated he added, 'Don't be afraid, I won't take advantage — I won't touch you. I like you a lot, but I want to know. You so often say Tony was — Tony did — always past tense.'

Her eyes met his honestly. 'There is no husband — now. I'm divorced.'

'I see,' he said, a little flatly.

'It was never a real marriage — it was just friends living together. We grew up together — married to please our parents. It was just an understood thing that we'd marry, and we were too young, too inexperienced.'

He looked interested. 'It's a relief to know I haven't to clear out to avoid a husband. What went wrong?'

'Tony did. He's not cut out for marriage. I was keen to continue police work at that time, but he wanted parties, night life, went somewhat girl-mad. Restless, discontented, we had no home, just rooms or a flat. His brother got into trouble as I told you, and I suddenly hated prison life and felt the cousin would be a drawback to that career having our name. Then I took up this illustrating and even that didn't suit Tony. He wanted me to gadabout with him, no ideas for a real home or family, which was all I wanted then and this illustrating. Teresa, my sister that was here, was more Tony's type and older than I am. They started going about together and I was left alone with my work. My own fault, I suppose. I accepted it, knowing who Tony had for a playmate, leaving me in peace. And then — ' Pauline halted, took a deep breath and finished, 'I found him in Teresa's bed.'

'The rat!'

'That was the end, of course. A good excuse to break up and go our own ways, but it knocked me back for a time — the deceit, the disloyalty. Yet

I was partly to blame, I should have seen where it was leading, that we were so unsuited, that Tony was so frivolous and undependable. We are still friendly, but the marriage was over. Teresa threw it all off and went away, picking up with other fellows, just as shallow and irresponsible as Tony — two of a kind. We had a terrific row at the time, Teresa and I, and when she left, casting off all the family, hurting Mother and Dad — there was no love left between us. Our parents were ill afterwards and needed help, so I went back home to look after them. That's my story, Dean. All in the past now.'

'You poor girl. What a time you had.'

'I'm contented now, Dean, happier than I've been for years.'

'I can understand you not wanting Teresa here, like something rotten gnawing at your peaceful life.'

'I suppose I was cruel — I was mad to think I could turn her out at that time of night — but I can't rid myself of the bitterness. She is still so selfish and demanding, takes all then laughs and leaves.'

'You *are* rather a mad person, you know,' he said gently. 'Taking a stranger like me into your home.'

She smiled at him. She had called herself mad that very afternoon. 'I've no regrets — I felt I could trust you. I feel free to do mad things now.'

'You funny girl.' He bent forward and patted her hand. 'But a nice girl, too.'

A few minutes later she said, 'I think I'll have to help you, Dean. You're getting nowhere like this. If you give me the address of — er — Bruce's rooms I'll call and see if I can find out where he is.'

'Oh, Pauline, could you — would you?' he exclaimed eagerly, then his smile faded. 'It's too much to ask. I can't involve you any further — I won't risk getting you into trouble.'

'I'm already involved, and there

needn't be any risk. I'll be most careful. I want to see you cleared of all this, and what can you do till you find your only alibi? You can't stick down in my dungeon — ' she smiled, — 'for the rest of your days.'

He laughed. 'It has its good points. There are far worse hardships.'

'Then I'll go tomorrow.'

'I'm going with you. Hide me in the boot or somewhere.'

'No, Dean, no. That's asking for trouble.'

'If they're still searching cars I'll skip out — I won't let them get me. They can shoot me first.'

'Oh no, Dean!' she exclaimed again.

'I need clothes, Pauline. If I can get back home — it's on the way — I'll sneak in and get some from my old room.'

'Your parents?'

'I won't see them. I'm not going to put them in danger. Mum is too timid, she'd let the cat out of the bag. I know how to get in all right.'

After a moment she nodded. 'Very well. We'll go to bed early and set off before dawn, while it is still dark.' As she moved about straightening the place for night-time, she said, '*Do* I know all about you, Dean? Did you live with your parents? Have you never been married?'

'I told you I worked with Dad and the house is there. When I wasn't moving around for wrestling matches and in digs, that was my headquarters. I'm not married and I've no girl friend. The girls made a fuss of me as a wrestler, but perhaps because of that — I never fancied one for keeps. I never met one like you before, Pauline, taking me on trust like this, taking me without the glamour of the ring.'

'You're too good-looking to be a wrestler,' she said candidly, studying his clear-cut face. 'I would never have guessed. No wonder the girls fell at your feet.'

8

Pauline awoke at three in the morning, was immediately wide awake and got up, putting on a warm dress as the early hours were chilly. It was quite still outside but dark except for a few twinkling stars. She woke Dean up then made coffee for them both, and packed a flask of more coffee and some food into her picnic basket. Dean was glad of the coffee but refused anything to eat.

'Let's get going, then,' she said. 'Carry all these rugs out for me, will you, Dean? We'll have to make you look like a bundle of old clothes or something.'

Rex wandered around them with a puzzled expression, bewildered by this sudden disturbance of his night's sleep. He paused doubtfully on the front step as Pauline opened the door to the chilly dark. Then as they made for the car he bounded down after them and leapt into his seat as soon as the car door was opened. 'He'll be a good guard,' said Pauline, with a smile. 'I don't think anyone will suspect me of carrying a runaway with him up front.'

'A convict. Don't be too kind, Pauline,' said Dean. 'It's a long drive,' he murmured, as she buried him under blankets, rugs and cushions.

'We'll make it in no time. There won't be much traffic for hours.'

Besides quiet roads with little traffic, only an odd lorry or two, there seemed no more signs of the police and their dogs. They were probably looking further afield for him by now, thought Pauline hopefully. Once safely away from a well-lighted town, back in the countryside and the first glimmer of dawn over the fields she drew up in a side road. 'Breakfast,' she said.

Dean came up for air and accepted some sandwiches and a mug of coffee. She let Rex out and gave him a drink, and when he returned to his seat gave him some of his biscuits to keep him happy.

'You've made good headway,' said Dean cheerfully.

'Yes. With luck I'll be knocking at Mrs Burley's door by seven o'clock. Will that be too early?'

'I shouldn't think so. She's always busy with lodgers. Bruce used to say she never seemed to go to bed.'

'Right. Settle down again, you two, and we'll be off.'

'You're a wonderful girl,' came Dean's muffled voice.

'Am I? That's nice to know.'

Dean's head shot out again. 'Are you in love with that man down your road?'

'Of course not.' She reversed the car sharply and shot down the outer road.

'Take care, love. Don't be had up for speeding.'

She laughed and cut the speed down. She drove steadily through awakening towns and the thickening of cars and buses, keeping a sharp look out for any police on the watch. Passing one or two on point duty was a bit of a strain, but except for an amused smile as they noticed Rex sitting there like a wise old man they showed little interest. As she had promised they passed Bruce Dunn's old rooms by seven o'clock. The front door to the porch was open and there was activity in the bay window downstairs. She drove up a quiet side road and got out of the car. 'Stay, Rex,' she ordered. She glanced at the still bundle of rugs in the back. A fine thing if a policeman came this way now and investigated. But perhaps Rex sitting up there like a statue with his indignant expression — because where she went he thought it his duty to follow her — perhaps that would satisfy anybody inquisitive. She turned quickly and went back to the house. The door was still open and one or two men emerging, apparently off to work. She went up the cracked steps.

'Is Mrs Burley anywhere about?' she asked a tall thin man in the dim, bacon-smelling hall.

'Hi, Ma!' the fellow shouted towards the rear. 'Someone wants you.'

'Your mother?' asked Pauline. Perhaps he could give her some information.

He grinned widely. 'Nah. She's Ma to all of us. A real good sort. I must be off, I'm late, so cheerio!'

As he sped down the steps a well-built woman, with a round rosy face and grey hair flattened down from a centre parting, came from the back. 'Yes, Miss? You're wanting rooms? I'm sorry, I don't take ladies. Place is full of gents, you know, and it wouldn't seem right to me,' she said, shaking her head.

'No, I'm looking for someone — an old friend. It's rather urgent. Does Bruce Dunn still live here?'

'Bruce — you mean the wrestler Battling Bruce? No, dear, we've lost him.'

'He's dead?' gasped Pauline, dismayed.

'Eh, I hope not, but I couldn't say. We haven't heard a word since — I don't know how long.' The woman's brow wrinkled. 'We've lost track of him. He went off to one of those wrestling matches, up Carlisle way, I think it was, and never a word or sight of him since.'

'It's very odd. I hoped you would know where he is. Well, thank you, Mrs Burley. I won't take up any more of your time.' Pauline turned to go.

'A pity being as you say he's wanted urgently. I tell you what, he left a case of his things here, a few shirts and things. How about you taking them with you. I don't reckon he'll be coming back here now.'

'I don't know whether I ought to.' Pauline hesitated, considering. Clothes for Dean, she thought.

'I don't think he'd mind as you're his friend. He can't be much bothered about them. I'd like them out of the way. You'll be finding him somewhere, no doubt.'

'I hope so, but it's difficult. All right, I'll take them. Does he owe you anything?' Surely she wouldn't part with his belongings if he did, thought Pauline.

'No, Bruce was always considerate. Always well in advance, so he could pop in and out just as he liked. I owe him some back if the truth be known. I let his room go. I could have always fixed him in somehow if he returned unexpectedly.' She smiled. 'It's an elastic sort of house.'

'They're lucky to have such an amiable landlady,' said Pauline.

When the large shabby suitcase was put at her feet she thanked the woman again and left the house, stumbling a little with the cumbersome suitcase. As Rex's tail thumped his seat and he whimpered a relieved welcome, she dropped the bag into the boot of the car.

'What on earth's that?' came Dean's voice from the floor.

'It's a suitcase of Bruce's, some

clothes of his. I thought they might fit you — that Bruce wouldn't mind.'

'Don't understand. Where's Bruce?'

'He's not there and they don't know where he is. We'll talk it over later, Dean.'

'Oh, lord!' As she climbed into the driving seat, he said, 'The clothes — a good idea. Bruce and I were much the same size. Perhaps we needn't call in at my old home after all.'

'I've no idea what's in the bag.'

'Draw in somewhere quiet and we'll have a look.'

'We'll have to get well away from here, it's getting busy.'

The car spurted away towards the main roads and they did not speak again for some time. What now? pondered Pauline. What a wasted journey. Bruce Dunn had simply faded into the blue. What could Dean do now? Without Bruce he was lost. Well away from towns and in the midst of fields and hedges she drew up in a lonely spot, let Rex out for a run and they opened the suitcase that fortunately was not locked. There were a few books and oddments, old letters, a hair-brush and toilet articles, some underclothes, a coloured shirt or two, a jersey, cardigan, a pair of well-worn shoes and shabby trousers, all pushed in casually, probably by Mrs Burley as she cleared his room.

'Well, well,' said Dean, turning the things over. 'These clothes will be a help. They'll put me on for a while. We'll drive straight back now and decide what to do next — that is, if all right with you, Pauline?'

She sighed. 'A pity we've run into a blank wall again. A wasted journey.'

'I wouldn't say that, at least we know Bruce left these parts, and I have a new outfit.' He grinned and took the mug of coffee she offered him. 'I'm glad of this. A bit dry and stifling under that heap of rugs.' He stuffed the letters and odd papers back in the suitcase. 'No help with those. Let's move on, Pauline. I feel sure something will turn up if you can put up with me a bit longer.'

He seemed more hopeful than she was. She whistled Rex back and they set off once more. She felt depressed, nothing was going their way. She had an uneasy feeling that it was going to be one of those days — they'd be lucky if they got back to the cottage without mishap. Her spirits dropped even lower as she saw a long dark car drawn up on her green, and walking down from the moors was her brother Harold. 'Oh, good heavens!' she gasped. 'That's all we need.'

'What is it now?' Dean peeped out of his coverings.

'More visitors.' She drove past and parked the car near the edge of the moors. 'My brother is here. This place is getting like a bus terminus. You'll have to lie low here. Go to sleep if you can to pass the time. Don't move if anyone comes — not till I speak to you. I'll get rid of them as soon as I can. Come on, Rex.'

She made sure all the doors were locked then hurried to the cottage. Harold's family were straggling down behind him from the sunny moors. She was sorry not feeling able to give him a welcome after so long a silence, but this time it was impossible. She had to harden her heart, because now, though being unable to explain it, she had merged her life with Dean's and she had no intention of giving him away.

'Whatever are you doing here, Harold?' she said, as the tall well-built fellow came up. Slowly behind him came his wife, Winnie, and the two blonde children, Henry ten years old, Sylvia eight years.

'You've been an age,' said Harold, as she unlocked the cottage door. 'We were here an hour or two ago.'

'You're lucky I'm back so soon. I nearly made a day of it.'

'Well, I suppose I should have phoned. I wanted to ask you — ' He looked back at his wife as she stood in the doorway. Rex was making friends with the children on the green. 'Will you do us a favour, Pauline? Win and I are going up to the Midlands — a conference. Will you put the kids up till we get back?'

Pauline turned cold. Things were getting worse — and poor Dean nearly suffocating on the floor of the car. 'I'm terribly sorry, Harold, but it's impossible. At the old house yes — but here I have no room for visitors. It's a one up one down sort of place. You'll have to ask someone else. You know plenty of people, you don't need me.'

'The kids don't mind camping. They'll sleep on the floor, in the bath — anywhere.'

'No, I'm sorry, Harold, but it's out of the question. I've a load of work on and — I'm tied otherwise — have engagements. I have all that to type out' — she waved a hand towards the clipped pages of Theo Gale's article.

'I can't understand you, Pauline. You never used to be so — so unfriendly. That affair with Tony has had a strange effect on you. They are good kids, wouldn't be any trouble.'

'Haven't I just said it's not convenient? You meant to dump them on me, just taking me for granted as usual. And how do I know what the children are like? I've only seen them once or twice since they were babies. You never brought them over, they never write. I've sent presents and never been thanked. You didn't take Teresa in, either — you sent her to me.'

'Well, really — what can one do for Teresa? And she and Win never get on.'

'You sent her to me. Why is it none of you ever bother about me, never helped with Mum and Dad — you only come when you want something. You can leave Tony out of it, too, he was more good-hearted than any of you in spite of his faults. Well, I'm waking up at last, just beginning to realize how you all use me. But not this time. I want to be free to get on with my work and mix with my own reliable friends.'

'Well, really — ' said Harold again. He glanced crossly at his wife still leaning up against the doorway. 'Why don't you come in and sit down, Win?'

'There seems no point,' she returned acidly.

We've never liked each other, thought Pauline, looking her over, her mousy hair and sulky mouth. It was her fault the children had been kept away.

'I'm disappointed. You've certainly changed, Pauline,' sighed Harold.

'*You* changed soon after you left home and became somebody in the town. I know how much your attitude hurt Mum and Dad. Coming to the funeral was too late, it could never make up for your neglect. Well, that's that — I've had my say.' Pauline turned away. 'I'll get you all a cup of tea or something, then I must be off — I have an appointment.'

'Don't bother,' said Harold, going towards the door. 'I wouldn't ask you for another thing. We'll drive off and get a meal somewhere.'

It all ended as frostily as it had begun. A day of home truths, thought Pauline, watching them leave. She was no doubt hard and cold but she was in the right. She would no longer harbour such bitterness at the shallowness of her family now she had spoken up and cleared the air. They collected their children and got into their large opulent-looking car. Yet it seemed dreadful to part like this from her own brother. Probably she would never see them again. The children had not even looked at her, all their interest was in the romping, lovable, cream-coloured dog. She was a stranger to them. Yet all her mind was on one man who was stealing into her lonely heart, on Dean lying uncomfortably in the close locked car. He seemed doomed to spend his days behind locked doors. She shrugged her shoulders, shaking the family off. They didn't matter. Her dislike of Winnie and disapproval of Harold had been building up over the years. As soon as the dust from their car settled and the only sound some bird song in the lilac tree, she went over to her own car.

'Be quick, Dean, while there's no one about. Leave the suitcase, I'll bring it.'

'Not this time. It's too bulky for you.' He snatched up the suitcase as though it were a feather-weight and dashed up to the cottage and inside. Relieved, Pauline followed and closed the door behind them.

'The lies I'm telling for you, Dean! They simply mount up. I just hope some good comes out of it all.'

'You've sent your people away. I'm sorry, Pauline. I think it's time for me to get out of your way.'

'No,' she said firmly. 'I'm determined to straighten this out if I can. We'll get a meal then think things over. As for my family — ' she looked back from the door to the rear steps — 'we've been breaking apart for some time. I suppose I've grown cold and nasty, but a person can put up with just so much, and I couldn't say anything while our parents were alive — for their sakes I tried to keep the peace.' She laughed uneasily. 'I'm afraid the worm has turned, as they say.'

'You cold and nasty, never! You wouldn't be doing all this for me if you were really so horrible. Though I must say you can be a very determined young woman when necessary.'

9

The meal over, neither Pauline nor Dean could settle, still in a quandary of what to do next. 'Sit down and read the paper, Dean. We'll be able to think clearer tomorrow. I'm going to get that article typed for my friend.' She uncovered her typewriter and drew Theo's papers towards her.

'A good idea,' agreed Dean. 'For the moment I'm stumped, and it's certainly homely and very comfortable here. Wish I need never leave.'

She smiled at him, her colour deepening. 'Do you?' she said softly.

'Goodness knows where I'd be now except for you.' He shook the newspaper open, but after a moment asked, 'Why are you doing all this for me, Pauline? Do you like me?'

Her eyes met his steadily. 'Yes, I like you — and believe in you, I don't know the reason why but I do — so don't let me down.'

'Pauline, when I'm cleared of all this, can I come back? Do you think it's possible for two people meeting like this — that something good might come out of it all?'

'Leave it, Dean,' she interrupted. 'It remains to be seen. We're all in the dark just yet.'

'Yes, that's true. I've no right to talk like that — an escaped convict — '

'Stop it, you've no right to say that, either. Don't think of yourself like that.'

'Sorry, Pauline. It's simply this frustration getting to me, I expect.' He turned over a few pages of the newspaper then looked up again, as though unable to concentrate. 'You know, Pauline, although I loathed prison and being locked away from the world, they were pretty decent to me there. I think some of the officers believed in me, especially one who was crazy on wrestling, used to talk to me about it and go and get glued to the T.V. whenever he could to watch it. I think, perhaps, if it hadn't been for them closing their eyes to certain things I wouldn't have got away so easily.'

'You'd better keep that to yourself in future,' she said. 'Don't let anyone think they weren't keeping an eye on you, it's only fair if they were — er — decent to you. Now forget that horrid place, Dean, and let me get on with some work.'

'Sorry, I'm a real pest, aren't I?' He buried himself in the newspaper at last and, except for the steady tapping of the typewriter there was silence for a time. Rex was fast asleep, making up for his disturbed rest, once or twice kicking in his sleep and muttering. Theo's article finished, Pauline worked on sketches for Vanessa's book for a while. Suddenly she pushed everything aside and stood up.

'I'll take this article down to Theo in the morning,' she said. 'I'm going to bed soon, Dean. I'm exhausted.'

'Yes, I'll go, too. It's been a long day,' he said, stifling a yawn.

And a wasted one, too, thought Pauline regretfully, glancing at her last picture of Mopsie and Muffit. Even her work seemed unsatisfactory, she had been unable to concentrate properly. She studied Dean's handsome head with its short clipped dark hair, as he finished the chapter of a book he had picked up. She had 'fallen' for him badly, the most astounding thing in her whole sensible, careful life, and dreaded letting him slip away from her. Everyone would call her a fool and point out the risk she had taken. She only had his word, supposing he really was a bad lot? Oddly enough she didn't care, she was ready to go along with him whatever he was. Other women had done stranger things . . .

He looked up suddenly, his blue eyes meeting hers directly. 'Now what are you planning in that lovely head of yours?'

She shook her head and turned away

to hide her tell-tale colour. 'I was just thinking — about the fix we are in.'

'A new day might bring something. Let's get to bed and sleep on it, Pauline.'

'That's all I feel capable of at the moment.' She yawned and went towards the inner door, only too ready to slip between the sheets.

* * *

The next day was again bright and tempting. 'I don't think we'll get better weather than this in July,' said Pauline, clearing the breakfast table. 'It's too early. We'll pay for it later.'

'I've been thinking,' said Dean. 'I must repay you in some way for all your goodness.'

'It's all right, Dean, plenty of time for that —'

'No. I can't do much, but I can do some gardening for you. I see there are some seeds waiting to be planted. It's time they were going in now.'

'Oh, would you, Dean?' Pauline's face brightened. 'I'd be so pleased. It's been on my mind, but I've had so many other things to see to, and Vanessa seems to think I have nothing else to do but illustrate her books.'

'It's an ideal day. I'll get the back dug over and the first seeds in.'

'My first job is to deliver that article, and then do some shopping. You'll be out of sight all right in the back.'

'Sure. Don't worry about me.'

'Have you thought of any plan yet? Supposing I called on some other people you know — isn't there a sort of wrestlers' association or something?'

'Keep away from that crowd, Pauline, they'd be on to me like hot cakes. They never tried to help me out before. They'd know you were hiding me — the police know well enough that someone is hiding me. Without Bruce I have no proof, whatever they think of me. Vincent and I came near to a fist fight in the ring, the referee had to drag us apart, but as for using a knife — me never! But you see you can't blame them for thinking the worst.'

'Well, go on making plans while you scatter little seeds,' she said, smiling. 'I won't be long. Come along, Rex. Dean can have you later.'

She stopped the car at Theo's gate. Mrs Elton came to the door. 'Sorry, dear, Mr Gale isn't in. He's taken a taxi to the station. His daughter Brenda is coming over. Some sort of school holiday for a few days.'

'How nice for him, but could he go and meet her? I mean, if he'd let me know — '

'He can't get to her quick enough. He adores that girl, Mrs Crompton.'

'Then will you put this packet on his desk, please, Mrs Elton. Tell him it's all typed and ready for posting, and I'll see him later. I expect Brenda will help him with it.'

'Yes, I'll tell him. Be sure to come down sometime, won't you? He'll be that keen to show off his daughter.'

'I'm looking forward to meeting her.'

Pauline turned to go.

'Are you wanting anything doing? I'll come if you want me.'

'Everything's all right yet, Mrs Elton, thank you. I've been out a lot so it keeps fairly tidy.'

'Well, all right if you think so. I'll be along someday soon.'

Pauline hoped it wouldn't be too soon, as she went back to the car. Poor Mrs Elton, she was just a bit too willing to 'do' for folks. She leant out of the car. 'Come along, Rex. No good sitting there, Bonny isn't at home.'

'Is he behaving?' Mrs Elton called, as the dog went to the gate, looked back with a puzzled expression — no doubt a wasted journey to his mind — then leapt lightly into his car seat.

'Of course he is,' laughed Pauline. 'He's the nicest dog I've ever known.'

'He's bound to be if he's a chip off Bonny's breed,' came the woman's last words.

Pauline was further dismayed when she reached the village. Both the grocery store and the post-office had an easily recognizable photograph of Dean Jameson plastered on their windows. HAVE YOU SEEN THIS MAN? ANY INFORMATION TREATED IN CONFIDENCE. GET IN TOUCH WITH YOUR POLICE STATION OR AT THIS NUMBER . . . it said in bold print, followed by a telephone number.

She did her shopping and rushed back to her cottage. Dean was still digging over the back garden, looking happy and energetic. His ankle was almost better, he hardly limped now. She went to the back door and beckoned him in.

'You'll have to lie low,' she said urgently. 'We can't do much yet. There are photos of you all over the place. They never give up, do they? I thought by now — '

'They must know someone is harbouring me, Pauline. Never mind, I'm not surprised. I can go on with the gardening. It's sheltered down here, but if anyone *should* spot me' — he grinned — 'you're a dab hand at story-telling.'

'Dean Jameson! You're making me into a thoroughly bad lot!'

'Give me half a chance,' he teased. 'I'll take you up on that.'

'Oh, go on! I'm going to get some work done.' She turned towards the steps inside. 'We'll have to be patient till this dies down, though we do seem to be wasting precious time.'

His smile faded. However much he joked and tried to be cheerful she knew he was worried about Bruce Dunn, and anxious about the predicament he was in, with no certainty of clearing his name. She went up to her work-table and managed to make up for the hours she had wasted yesterday. Rex was in the garden with Dean, getting in the way, scuffling in the turned earth with soil on his nose, intrigued by an occasional worm. They came indoors some time later, looking warm and tired.

'That's most of the seeds in — if

the pooch will let them be,' said Dean, slapping the dog's backside. 'I'll finish tomorrow. How's your work gone on?'

'Very well. I think a break from it has done me good.'

'Fine. I'll go and get these overalls off and into Bruce's old trousers.' He paused by the door. 'That garden below is a sun-trap. You could grow grapes, peaches — anything, I guess.'

She smiled. 'If you are still here next Spring we'll consider it.'

'Don't encourage me with such promises, love,' he chaffed, and went off downstairs.

As Pauline straightened up her pages, clipping coloured illustrations into the appropriate places, Dean came back washed and brushed, in the brown trousers and a shirt as blue as his eyes. 'I feel a new man,' he said cheerfully.

She laughed. 'You look very smart, Mr Jameson.'

'You'd be surprised how different it makes one feel after prison clobber.'

Work done, they enjoyed the rest

of the evening together, finding they had many interests in common, finding pleasure in books and television, and discovering they both liked doing crosswords. Pauline unearthed Scrabble from her store cupboard and the evening fled by contentedly, both of them forgetting for a space the cloud they were living under.

He took her hand as she put his bedtime drink down beside him and kissed it. 'I'm getting too fond of you, Pauline. Lock me in tonight.'

'I'll do no such thing — you've had too many locked doors — but — ' she smiled at him — 'I'll lock myself in to satisfy you.'

As she curled up in bed the thought struck her that he was free to go any time with no locked doors against him. Yet she knew he wouldn't. He was happy here, he wouldn't risk getting caught for both their sakes. Somehow they had to be sensible and think out a plan, but what? The future for him all looked so black and impossible.

10

The next day or so passed by just as pleasantly. Dean took on household duties while she made good headway with the illustrating. Washing up, taking the vacuum around, peeling potatoes, anything to help her. She laughed as the vacuum died into silence at last. 'Who needs Mrs Elton?' she said, then frowned. 'That reminds me, we must keep an eye open for her. I'm afraid no one could undo our good work more than Mrs Elton.'

For a breath of fresh air, much needed, Pauline took Rex for walks on the moors, yet she was uneasy, unable to feel her usual pleasure in the fine sunny weather and healthy, earthy smells of gorse and other wild growing things. All that open space yet she felt as though she were being watched from every hollow or scrubby bush. She soon returned, finding that picking up her pencils and pens and getting absorbed in her work was more relaxing than anything.

'I'm getting nervy,' she thought, as a knock at the front door one morning nearly shot her out of her chair. 'This is stupid.'

Without thinking she opened the door and smiled at the young girl standing there. A pretty young thing with the deepest of blue eyes below a fringe, and straight thick brown hair to her shoulders. Pauline tried to remember — somewhere she had seen the girl before.

'Hello,' the girl said, smiling. 'I'm Brenda — Brenda Gale.'

'Oh, of course. I felt I knew you, though I've only seen your photograph. Do come in, I'm so glad to meet you. You are very much like your dad.'

'He's a real pet, isn't he?' Brenda said, following Pauline inside. 'He's told me a lot about you. I'd love to see some of your illustrations. Of course, I've seen some of Vanessa Dorne's books. I read sometimes to the young ones in their class.'

She was greatly interested and amused by the colourful pictures of Mopsie and Muffit, and then by the unusual shape of Lilac Cottage. 'Dad used to talk about this place and Ben who lived here, but somehow I never got here. I think Dad kept me away on purpose because you see, they had no children, there was something sad — '

'Yes, your dad told me, they were an unfortunate couple in many ways. Now, Brenda, let's have some morning coffee.'

Downstairs, Brenda suddenly exclaimed. 'Oh, you've got a gardener!' Pauline had forgotten about Dean. He was plainly visible from one of the downstairs windows, busy cutting back and trimming some growing plants that somehow managed to thrive through the back rock face.

'Well, yes,' she said slowly. 'Just to get the garden into shape. Afraid I'm not much of a gardener. I love flowers but I hate to destroy anything, and let things grow till I'm sure they are weeds and not a valuable plant.'

'I'm sure Dad could do with help in the garden. The old gardener is ill — if you could get this man to help him — '

'We'll see — ' said Pauline hesitatingly. 'I know he is very busy, but I'll see what he says.'

'Thank you for helping Dad with the typing,' Brenda said, as they sat drinking their coffee. She dived into a packet of chocolate wafer biscuits. 'I shouldn't really, should I? But I love these.'

'I think your dad is a very brave man, carrying on through all his difficulties.'

'I think he and Mother will get together again, you know,' said Brenda confidently. She was a curious mixture of youthfulness and maturity, from one to the other in a second. 'Mother is a lovely person.' As Pauline was silent, she added, 'She made a mistake. I know she regrets leaving Dad and is too ashamed to come back. She has been ill, fretting about it, but she doesn't want him to know or feel pity for her. But I'll get them together one day.'

'Persuade her to bury her pride and come back,' said Pauline, knowing she had expected this herself some day. 'I know he still loves her and wants her.'

'Yes, he has never blamed her. We can't really blame her, either, can we? His blindness was a great shock to them both, but she has changed. She's no longer happy going about without Dad — she got bored with too much of her — friend. She and Dad had something — they belong together, and someday soon I'll manage it.'

'If there's anything I can do — '

Brenda smiled again, her whole face lighting up. 'It will happen, you'll see.'

Pauline, captivated by the strength and assurance overriding the girl's fresh young innocence, knew it would, too.

She wished her own affairs were as clear and straightforward. 'I'll walk down with you,' she said, as Brenda rose to go. 'I haven't seen Theo for a day or two. I'll fetch Rex.'

'Oh, yes, you've got a great-grandson of Bonny's, haven't you?'

'Something like that. He's a lovable creature.' Pauline went down to the back door. 'Come along, Rex, walkies!' As Dean looked up she said quietly, 'I'm just going down the road. Won't be long.' She went across to him. 'You've been spotted — you are now my gardener and in danger of getting another job.'

He frowned. 'Who?'

'A young girl, the daughter of my friend Theo down the road. Don't worry — it will pass over. Come along, Rex, come and see Bonny.'

'So my little girl found you,' said Theo delightedly, his arm about his daughter's slim shoulders. 'You must tell me what Pauline is like, Brenda. I've only got my guesses and her voice, and Mrs Elton's descriptions to go on, and you know how muddled she gets.'

'She's pretty and so nice, Dad, but I'll tell you all you want to know later. Just now I'm going to see how lunch is getting on.'

'I'm not stopping,' said Pauline quickly. 'I only came down to see how you were, Theo. I've been busy and rather neglected you.'

'Oh, you must stay,' said Brenda, and disappeared in the direction of Mrs Elton and kitchen sounds.

'Of course you are staying,' said Theo firmly. 'You can leave straight afterwards if it's urgent.'

'I'll do that, then, if you don't mind. Vanessa Dorne is likely to be coming over. If you've any more typing to do let me take it with me. Theo, Brenda is a lovely girl, you might well be proud of her, and somehow so grown-up and sensible for her age.'

'Poor girl, so much was thrust upon her. My misfortunes robbed her of her baby life, I'm afraid.'

'I'm glad you've got each other.'

He sighed. 'Yes. The days are so different when she is here. So much more chatter, laughter and music. There *is* some more typing, Pauline, if you wouldn't mind. All the same, I shouldn't bother you —'

'It is no bother. I'm interested and like to do it, Theo, so let me have it now, and then I won't forget to take it when I go.'

She watched silently as he walked over to his desk and with wonderful precision opened the drawer, moved one or two things and picked up a large envelope, from the exact position he had left it. As he brought it over to her, he said unexpectedly, 'What's the matter, Pauline? You seem worried about something. I've felt it before. There's something on your mind.'

How perceptive he was! She ought to have known he would sense something. Again she wished she could tell him and ask his advice. 'I'm a bit worried about a friend of mine. He's got into difficulties. I wish I could tell you, but he's confided in me, and it's all rather a private affair. I'm not free to tell you — '

'Not the ex-husband?'

'Oh no, nothing to do with Tony. Sometime I'll tell you all about it. I could do with your advice, but I'm unable to talk about it.'

'Well, if I can help any time let me know. I'll treat everything in confidence.'

'I'm sure you would. Perhaps soon I'll be able to explain it all.' She hesitated a moment then ventured, 'Part of it — Theo, do you believe in love at first sight?'

'So that's it! There's another man in your life.'

'As I said, it's part of it, but I'm so afraid of making a mistake again. I've never — known anything like this before — but is it just infatuation? What do you think, Theo?'

'I know it can happen because that

is how it was with Valerie and me. We met on a boat trip and at once it was snap — like the click of a camera. It was a wonderful thing, yet we have parted, it wasn't strong enough to bring us through our difficulties so we are a poor example. How can I advise you?'

'Yet it can happen. You had some wonderful years of happiness, and I feel that will count — I'm sure it's not the end of you two. You'll come together again.'

He sighed again. 'It's a lovely thought, but I wouldn't want to burden Valerie — as I am now.'

'People change, more settled as they grow older. You are too unselfish, Theo. You can do so much, so clever in spite of your blindness that we forget all about it. You would be no burden.'

'Then I hope your dreams come true — for both of us. And now here comes lunch.'

Preceded by spicy, tempting food

smells, Brenda and Mrs Eton carried trays of eatables in. The girl's face was beaming. 'There's a special sort of salad,' she announced. 'I hope you'll like it and the soup I've made. I've got a new cookery book and Mrs Elton is teaching me a lot.'

'You couldn't have a better teacher,' Pauline said.

'I'm thinking of coming over to you tomorrow, Mrs Crompton,' said Mrs Elton.

Pauline sought for a quick excuse. 'Leave it for a while, will you, Mrs Elton? I'll be away from home. I have a few journeys to make, to the publishers and so on — '

The woman sniffed disapprovingly. 'All right, but you know how dusty and cobwebby a place gets even with no one in it, and that pup running in and out . . . '

Pauline turned her attention to the soup. No matter what she said, Mrs Elton would have the last word. 'Well, let me know just as soon as you can,' added the woman, and went back to the kitchen. Pauline felt uncomfortable. Did Mrs Elton or Theo think she didn't trust the woman to work in the cottage when no one else was there? But Dean *was* there, and so they'd have to think what they liked.

'Don't let her worry you,' put in Theo quietly, 'She means well, but she does get on top of you at times. All the same she's a good sort and I couldn't do without her.'

'It's only that I'm a bit disturbed at the moment, over private affairs as I told you, Theo. Please explain to Mrs Elton, I don't want to upset her.'

'It would take more than that to upset her.'

'Dad,' said Brenda, eager to change the subject, 'Pauline has found a gardener. What about him helping you out?'

'Oh, Brenda, I can't promise he'll come,' said Pauline. 'He's up to his eyes in work, and they are very independent these days, aren't they? He doesn't live in the village. A friend sent him, knowing I'd had no chance to do the garden yet, so I was very lucky.'

'Try and talk him into it, Pauline,' said Theo. 'I could do with him. It's only till old Berny comes back, as I hope he will when he gets his legs back.'

Pauline felt she was getting deeper and deeper into a morass of falsehoods, they just mounted up, and she was glad when Brenda found something else more interesting to talk about. She always had a store of news for her father, knowing how cut off he was from the world these days.

As Pauline left Theo's cottage, Sergeant Willing from their little police station was cycling up the lane. She waited for him, knowing him as part of their village as everyone did. 'Sit, Rex!' she commanded, and to her delight for the first time after all her practice on the road he obeyed. Perhaps he had some respect for this blue uniform after all, she thought whimsically. The sergeant touched his cap, smiling, and got off his bicycle.

'Good afternoon, Mrs Crompton. Are you settling in all right?' He nodded up towards Lilac Cottage.

'Yes, I like it very much and feel as though I've been here years. It's like home to me.'

'Good. You've got a grand dog there, too.'

'Yes, he's a lovable pet. A bit too boisterous yet, but I'm trying to teach him to behave. He's only young.'

'He's shaping well. That breed make good, intelligent companions.' He said, fondling the dog's head. 'It's wise to have a guard dog, you're in a lonely spot, yet that doesn't seem to worry you.'

She smiled. 'Not at all. I'm used to coping by myself, and I can have friends calling if I get lonely.'

He paused by the gate to her cottage, Rex licking his hand. 'I've always had a fancy for this cottage, rather envy you possessing it.'

'Some say it's a peculiar shape.' Pauline's eyes passed over the windows. Where was Dean?

He laughed. 'That's what I like about it. I don't like places built exactly brick by brick, all the same like matchboxes. Sometime will you let me have a look inside? I haven't seen it properly since I saw them blasting out the rock and building this. An ingenious idea building into the rock like this. Mrs Elton has talked about it and I've always been really curious about it.'

Pauline's knees trembled. She hoped he hadn't seen any change in her. Thrusting back her shoulders, she pushed open the gate bravely. 'How about now, then?' Take the bull by the horns . . . She trusted Dean was hidden by now.

'Thanks all the same, but I must move on. Standing here gossiping, and I've got an appointment up on the moor. I'll keep you to your promise, though, one day.' He swung up on to his bicycle. 'I like to get to know any new-comers to our village. I'm here to help you all if you are in any trouble.'

'Thank you, I'll remember.' He smiled back at her and went on up the stony hill. So Mrs Elton had been talking. That little old busybody!

She rushed indoors hot with anxiety, but was not surprised to find the big room empty of any occupant. 'Dean!' she called, and sank into a chair breathlessly, as though she had run up the lane without a break. 'Go and find Dean, Rex.'

A few moments later Dean ran up the steps, Rex springing at his heels. 'Pauline, whatever are you doing, bringing that copper here? I think my heart has dropped down into my boots somewhere.'

'How do you think *I* feel? I didn't bring him, he was coming up the road behind me. It would have looked suspicious if I'd ignored him. We all know and like him. Anyway, you're darn lucky, he was for coming in to have a look round.'

'What? Pauline, he must have guessed something — '

She shook her head. 'No, he's as innocent as a babe. He just has a fancy for this cottage, heard about it, saw it being built, all looking so extraordinary, etcetera.'

'My goodness!' Dean sank into a chair and cuddled Rex's forelegs and chest across his knees. 'I could see the cell door closing on me again.'

'I'm sorry, Dean, but it was a sticky situation.' She smiled wryly. 'It seemed wiser to brave it out, to prevent him thinking anything was out of the ordinary. Have you had anything to eat? I was practically forced to stay down there for lunch.'

'That's all right, I mustn't disrupt your life any more than I can help. I had a jam-butty, so I can wait!'

'I'll get you something.' She got up out of the chair. 'Dean,' she said from downstairs, 'we'll have to do something, I feel our luck is running out. I hate telling all these lies, too, especially to my friends. It can't last, someone is going to get suspicious.'

'I know, my dear,' he said, coming down after her, 'and I hate getting you so involved like this. In a day or two if we can't think what to do, I'll clear out. I'll disguise myself and disappear overseas. Other men have done it and gone for good. It's worth a try.'

'Oh no, Dean — ' Tears sprang to her eyes. She looked stricken. The love of her life, to lose him like that — so soon, too.

His arm across her shoulders, he said, 'I could always send for you after a safe length of time, if you still wanted my company. I'd have a different name and look different, of course. I'd shave all my hair off, if you like, do a Yul Brynner.'

She laughed shakily. 'For heaven's sake, don't do that. I hope it won't come to fading away like that. Dean, I can't let you do it — '

'Well, we won't worry about it for

a day or so. Let's enjoy life while we can.' He moved away from her. 'I can't say all I'd like to say to you, Pauline. I think such a lot of you, but I must be a free man first. Now what's that you've got for me? Looks tempting.'

'It's only a poached egg, you silly man,' she laughed. 'We'll have a dinner tonight.'

'Looks good enough to eat,' he chaffed. 'Come on, love, let's be happy for the rest of the day — forget about Bruce and everybody.'

11

Saturday afternoon came round again, all work done and time to relax. Pauline and Dean were happy together though no nearer a solution to their problems. The gardening was finished for a while, and Dean had done some repairs, such as loosening a stiff drawer and mending a catch on a cupboard door. Pauline had finished and delivered her illustrations and collected more work to do, to cover her word to Mrs Elton. Vanessa had spoken of dropping in again one day, and Pauline hoped Dean would be somewhere safe by then — yet how she would miss him! Except for a shower or two of rain the weather was quite delightful, and she would have loved a stroll over the moors with Dean and Rex. She wondered, when he was really free, if he would ever care to walk that way, despite the fresh scents and lovely colours, without thinking of those grim walls some miles ahead.

'Pauline,' he said suddenly, breaking into her thoughts, 'do you mind if we watch the wrestling? I'd like to see who is top of the programmes these days.'

'Why, of course. It's natural you'd like to see it. Remind you of old times.'

He sat with his eyes glued to the television set, making odd comments now and again, recognizing one or two of the 'boys'. 'That's a new young chap,' he said once. 'Don't know him. Speedy, just what I like. Full of tricks.' As the second bout came on, he said, 'I don't care for Magnificent Maurice. Too fond of tossing them out of the ring. Only wins that way, I guess. Just look at him now — that was a crafty punch.'

Pauline watched him as he sat there, leaning eagerly forward. It reminded her of Tony — the hours he had spent watching wrestling, trying to get her interested and drag her away from her needlework or sketching. She sat up suddenly. 'Tony!'

Dean looked around in astonishment. 'What is it? The husband that was? You haven't seen him there on T.V., have you?' He laughed. 'I'm jealous.'

'No, I've just thought — if anyone knows anything about the wrestlers it's Tony. He follows all sport, the form of players, everything. I'm going to phone him. He'll know where that Bruce fellow is. Why didn't I think of it before?'

'That sounds hopeful.' Dean's face brightened. 'You don't mind phoning him?'

'Of course not. We parted friends, and we grew up together, remember? When the wrestling and results are over I'll ring up. I only hope he hasn't gone away to a match of some sort.'

As soon as she felt Tony would have finished with the sport programme, Pauline went to the telephone.

'Pauline? Well, surprise, surprise!' came Tony's cheerful voice over the wires. 'What has brought this on?'

'Tony, have you been watching wrestling?'

'Naturally, love. You know I don't like to miss it.'

'Can you tell me about one of them? Where has that — er — Battling Bruce got to? There seems no sign of him these days.'

'Don't tell me you've gone mad on wrestling at last! It seems to get the ladies in time — beautiful bodies and all that . . . '

'No, I want to know for a friend. He wants to find him — it's rather urgent.'

'A friend — so you've found a boyfriend after all, have you, sweet Pauline? About time, too.'

'Be serious, Tony. I wouldn't ask you but it's important for him to know. Where is the man?'

'Let me see now . . . ' She could imagine him pushing his hand through his crisp fair hair as he thought. 'Battling Bruce — of course — he isn't wrestling any more. He's out. He was in a bad car crash, long time ago now — on the way to Carlisle, I think it was. He was in a coma for ages afterwards, they gave him up at first, but now he's slowly recovering. But he won't be wrestling any more.'

'A car crash. That explains it,' breathed Pauline. 'Where is he now?'

'He's in a convalescent home somewhere. I'm not sure where.'

'We have to find him. Is there any way we can find out, Tony?'

'I don't know what all this is about, but look — Pauline, I'll find out for you. He used to have a mate along with him — a lot seemed to go wrong just then. I'm trying to remember . . . '

'Yes,' said Pauline hurriedly, 'but never mind about him. Do me a favour and find Bruce, will you? You know a lot of those fellows — someone must know.'

'I'll find him all right. I'll ring you back, Pauline, as soon as I know.'

'Thanks Tony. I — we'd be very

grateful. I'll explain later.'

'Pauline,' he broke in, as she was about to ring off, 'has Teresa been to see you?'

'Yes, she was here.'

'She came pestering me just because her latest has got bored with her. I know I'm no angel, but she's a little vixen, Pauline. Keep her away from your boyfriend.'

'I packed her off — she won't be back.'

'It's all she deserves. 'Bye, Pauline. I'll be in touch soon.'

'Goodbye, Tony, and thanks.' Pauline hung up and turned to Dean. 'I think we're on the right track now. If Tony can't help I don't know who can.' She sat down and told him about all that had happened to Bruce Dunn. 'No wonder he never turned up to help you,' she said.

It was next day before Tony phoned. 'The dickens of a job, Pauline, but I've done it. Bruce is at Morston Court Nursing Home, out Hampstead Heath way. I managed to speak to him on the phone. He's had a tough time and will be something of an invalid for life by my enquiries, says Lyle knows of no lady who'd want to visit him, especially as he is now. He's a lonely person, guess he'd be glad of a friend. I hastened to tell him it's a friend of yours who actually wants to see him, business or something. So he said okay if he can be of any help. Visiting days are Wednesdays and Sundays, afternoons, two to four o'clock. Sunday today but you're too late now. It will have to be next Wednesday.' He stopped for a deep breath. 'Phew, what a mouthful!'

'Is he quite sensible? Can he remember the past if we talk to him about important things?'

'There's nothing wrong with him there. It's his chest and limbs, a battered leg, I think.'

'Would they mind if we went tomorrow? Tony, this is urgent.'

'The woman at the desk sounded

a bit of a dragon. Better make it Wednesday, ducks.'

'Well, we'll see. Thanks a lot, Tony. I thought you'd do it.'

'Let me know the outcome of it, won't you? Not like you to deal in mysteries.'

'Later, Tony. You'll be surprised at what comes out of this.'

'I've given over being surprised by what you do. You're a determined little creature when you start.'

'Well, thanks, Tony — '

'Pauline — '

'Yes?' as he hesitated.

'I wish you all the luck in the world — with the new love. You deserve it — after the way we treated you — '

'Goodbye, Tony.' She put the receiver down before he could say more. He was in one of his sentimental moods. She could hear the regret in his voice, but she would never trust him again. She had shut her eyes to a lot of his flirtations before, but never again. She told Dean what Tony had found out.

'Shall we chance going tomorrow?' she asked.

'A day or two can't hurt,' he said. 'We'll have more hope of seeing him in proper visiting hours. What a relief to know something! What a brain-wave of yours, Pauline.'

'I don't know why I didn't think of it before. Tony is sport mad. It was part of our disagreement. I was so bored with football matches, rugby, boxing and wrestling. He even pored over golf and tennis — everything. It was — is — a mania with him.'

'He could have done worse things.'

She smiled. 'And he did. He's an attractive man, Dean. He'd get round anybody.'

'I'll be everlastingly grateful to him for this. I hope to thank him in person someday soon. What are you smiling at?'

'When he knows about me linking up with a wrestler,' laughed Pauline. 'It will make his day.'

'Linking is a good word. I hope

it means we'll always be linked up together. There, you're making me say things I shouldn't till I'm straightened out.'

'It's because we're so relieved, Dean. At last we can get a move on.'

'Yes, roll on Wednesday. I feel like celebrating.' He stretched his arms luxuriously. 'What a pity we can't have a night out.'

She smiled again. 'Do you really want that?'

He shook his head. 'No. On second thoughts I'd rather be at home and happy with you.'

'In that case to celebrate if you must — I think there's at least some sherry in the sideboard.'

'Then what are we waiting for?'

As the evening before, the hours passed pleasantly by. As though free at last of niggling doubts, Pauline slept soundly that night, and was in a blissful mood next morning, bustling about with housework. So she experienced a nasty shock as she was sweeping and dusting around the front door in the warm sunshine, when Mrs Elton came through the gate and patted Rex as she approached.

'I see you are at home today after all, Mrs Crompton,' she said, passing by her into the room. 'I thought you might be and it suits me better today.'

Pauline could have hit the woman with the keen little bird-face. One could have too much of Mrs Elton. The woman paused just inside. 'Oh, you have your brother here.'

Dean, who had taken it upon himself to dust the book-shelves and straighten the books, stood staring at her, discomfited, caught out like a small boy. Pauline came inside after her. 'Not my brother, Mrs Elton — a cousin.'

'I see.' The woman's tone was strange. She looked Pauline over almost accusingly. Men about the place. A gardener on the quiet, now a cousin. Some women couldn't do without a fellow about the place. A pity, and she had seemed a nice girl, too . . . Pauline could see her little mind ticking over. 'Thought I had seen him before so took him for your brother. Thought there must be a likeness. Well, I'll start, if you don't mind, Mrs Crompton.'

'I hardly know what — I've just done this room.' Pauline looked at Dean, sick at heart. This was one thing she had hoped to avoid. He had discarded duster and books and had dropped into a chair, hidden behind the morning's newspaper.

'I'll go downstairs and see what there's to do there, then. Don't look so bothered, Mrs Crompton. I don't mind what I do.'

'You could clean the cooker or the bathroom — '

'Yes, I'll have a look round.' Giving Dean a look of despair, Pauline followed the woman downstairs. 'I see you've found the key to the store-room. That's a place I can clean up.' The busy little woman went into Dean's makeshift room.

'I had to put the camp bed up for my

cousin last night,' Pauline said hastily. 'He'll be leaving this evening.'

'This place needs straightening up all right. I'll take the bed down, then, if he's leaving.'

'Well — ' Pauline was lost for words, sick of lies.

'These old overalls, Mrs Crompton — ' Mrs Elton picked up the disreputable damp overalls from the floor in a corner.

'Put then in the dustbin, Mrs Elton. They're not worth keeping. My cousin wore them in the garden — putting seeds in.'

'I won't get in your way,' Mrs Elton said. 'An hour or two then I'll be off. Perhaps you have to go somewhere after lunch as you said.'

'It would be more convenient. Are you going to Mr Gale's?'

'Not today. I don't usually Mondays. He has plenty of food ready in, and Brenda is there just now to do for him. I know you didn't expect me today, but I won't be able to get up for a while — have to keep seeing to my old sick auntie, you know. Haven't you got some of your drawing to do? Don't let me bother you.'

'I've about finished but I'll go and put it together ready for delivering.' Somehow she must appease the too-willing woman, thought Pauline. 'Mrs Elton, before you go, could you make us one of your famous omelettes for lunch? You've made me greedy for them.'

The woman's little sharp eyes glittered. 'Of course, dear. Only too pleased. He's quiet, isn't he?' She nodded towards the upper floor.

'He's rather worried,' said Pauline quietly. 'He has troubles. He came to me for help.' At last, she thought wryly, a word of truth.

'He's lucky to have someone to turn to. Now I'll get on and keep out of your way.'

Pauline went upstairs, the dog behind her. He liked to be with Dean, and his curiosity over Mrs Elton's doings below now proved uninteresting. She shut the door and went over to Dean.

'Dean, I'm not waiting for Wednesday,' she murmured. 'I've had enough of this — it's getting on top of us. I'm not going to risk waiting. Early to bed tonight and we'll set off in the early hours.' She laughed. 'You'll have to put your bed up again — she's pulling it down.'

He grinned. 'Never mind. Let's keep her happy and get her off the premises.'

As half-past twelve approached Pauline set the table ready and Mrs Elton came up with the omelettes filled with some tasty smelling ingredients. 'There you are,' she said, putting the hot plates down in their places. 'And I hope the young gentleman will enjoy it.'

'I know he will, no doubt about that,' said Pauline.

Mrs Elton looked doubtfully at Dean who, after a muttered thanks, was bending over doing something unnecessary to his shoes. She probably thought he was a glum young man.

'I think I ought to have passed you off as dumb or deaf,' said Pauline, as the gate shut at last behind the woman. 'She must have thought you rather odd, and perhaps soon she'll start remembering. I hope she goes straight home to her cottage and stays there today.' She looked anxious. 'It's a bit of a scramble but perhaps we ought to get off at once . . . '

'We'll have a few hours sleep and get off through the night. We'll trust to luck, Pauline, it's all worked well so far. I'll see I'm not here if your friendly copper comes back — so don't you worry.'

'Very well. After I've cleared the dishes away I'll do Theo's typing for him and take Rex down there. I'll have to leave him. We might be London way a few days, I expect.'

'I'll wash up, you get on with the typing.'

'You'll find everything shining bright down below. At least we can't complain of Mrs Elton's cleaning methods.

There's not much of her, but when she works she works.'

'Strong as a horse,' muttered Dean, gathering plates together. 'And just as unpredictable.'

Indeed, Pauline's last glance around downstairs had shown her the bathroom and kitchen equipments sparkling white, and in the store-room the boxes had been piled tidily, the blankets folded and taken away, and the floor swept and scrubbed. The article neatly typed, Pauline packed up some of Rex's favourite food and biscuits, and took the dog down to Moor Cottage.

'I have to go to London for a day or two, so do you mind looking after Rex?' she asked, as Brenda came to the door, Theo close behind her.

'We'll have him, of course. Always glad to help, aren't we, Brenda?' said Theo, stooping to pat Rex as the dog brushed against his legs looking for Bonny. 'Bonny will take care of him. Something unexpected turned up, Pauline?'

'Yes, some stupid business. No, I won't come in, I have a lot to do before I set off. I'll get back as soon as I can.' Pauline smiled at Brenda and her father. 'Mrs Elton came to clean around. She saw my gardener, Theo — '

'*Did* she!'

'Yes. She was terribly curious as usual, but I didn't tell her much. She took him for a cousin — didn't seem so pleased to see a man in my cottage.'

Theo laughed. 'I'll probably hear about it. Thanks for the warning.'

Pauline left soon afterwards, not daring to look back at Rex, his collar being held by Brenda, and she heard the yelp of protest as the door closed. Already he thought he owned her and that nobody should be allowed to come between them. She knew he would be pained and worried at her leaving him behind, but she hoped he would soon settle down with Bonny and peaceful Theo Gale.

12

Sleep was the next thing for Pauline and Dean, after packing an overnight bag and small necessities for herself. Some hours later they got up, had a snack and stocked up the picnic-basket, then left the cottage in the calm, moonlight night.

'You'd better ride underneath as before,' Pauline decided. 'Come up for air in the open country and dive under before reaching any town.' She put their baggage and picnic-basket on the back seat beside him. 'A pity we haven't Rex with us this time to draw attention away from us. We'll have to disguise you as soon as I can get near a theatrical shop I know. I'll get some hairy stuff for a moustache and we must buy a cap to cover you up a bit. Here, try these dark glasses of mine on. Yes, fine. Those will do for a start.

You can hardly walk into that nursing home as you are. You'd be arrested on the spot.'

'What about Bruce, though?' said Dean.

'We'll meet that when we come to it. I want to test his memory first.'

'You think of everything, don't you, my dear?'

'I've taken charge of you, so I'll finish the job.'

'You've got guts, I'll say that for you. Someday — oh no, too early for me to make promises. Now, if you don't mind, I'll drop off to sleep again.'

'A good idea,' she murmured enviously. He slid under the covers and they drove in silence for some time. It was a beautiful night and rarely any traffic, and she could have thoroughly enjoyed driving if it hadn't been for their constant anxiety. As dawn was breaking she drew into a lay-by and they had breakfast. 'Seems funny without Rex,' she said again. 'That dog has become part of my life.'

'Wish I meant as much,' he sighed.

She smiled teasingly at him. 'How do you know you don't? I'll certainly miss you when I leave you behind with Bruce.'

'I'm not likely to stay in the home with him.'

'No, but you'll be under his wing once we've explained everything.'

'It's a vast relief to know he's still in the land of the living. I just hope he can remember — that night.'

'He will — he must, Dean. We can't have done all this for nothing.' Her tone told him it meant their future happiness. He smiled and nodded, buoyed up with fresh hope. They rested for a while because Pauline didn't want to get near the shops she had her mind on too soon, then she drove steadily on, taking no chances. They mustn't be held up for anything now — so near to success. Nearing their destination by midday she stopped by a village fish and chip shop and went in to buy a packet for each of them. Half a mile further on they stopped again to eat the contents and drain off the rest of the coffee in the flask. Later still she called in at a small, odd-looking man's shop and bought a checked grey cap.

'A bit countrified,' she said, as he put it on. 'How's that? It makes a difference already with those glasses.'

'It's too big,' he said, swivelling the peak round over his ears.

'I'll settle that when we get to the theatrical shop.'

'What have you had to do with theatricals?'

'Teresa was keen at one time, in the amateurs. She used to send up here for stage clothes and things, I've collected a few gee-gaws for her on hire. One of her crazes for a time.' Pauline laughed. 'She even raked Tony in once for the *Maid of the Mountains*.'

They came to the shop in question soon afterwards. Pauline came out from there with a small bag, and went back to the quiet road where she had left Dean in the car. She pushed a dusty-looking light brown wig over his head, and deftly stuck whiskers about his face. He sneezed, laughingly protesting. When she had finished he was disfigured by the rough wig and his face swathed in a whiskery beard and moustache. With the uncomely cap crowning all she laughed merrily. 'Your own mother wouldn't know you now.'

He looked in the driving-mirror, stroking the beard with a vain gesture. 'How do you like me now?'

'I don't. So don't ever think of growing a beard.'

Sitting beside her in the car, now feeling confident under his disguise, they went on the last tricky part of their journey. A little too confidently. Pauline's heart sank as a policeman suddenly signalled her to stop. She looked up at him questioningly. She couldn't have spoken to save her life, her tongue seemed rooted to the top of her mouth.

'Don't you know, Miss? This is a one-way street,' he said.

'Oh!' Pauline drew a deep breath, and looked about her anxiously. 'Last time I came this way — '

'Yes, no doubt it's been altered since, to save congestion of traffic, you know. A few streets about here have been altered. You ought to have noticed, though. Plenty of signs about.'

'I'm sorry.' He was looking curiously at Dean. 'And my cousin can't see very well, so he wouldn't notice. I'm sorry.'

'Yes, well — instead of backing all that way, drive up that back entry and turn right. You'll get on to the main road there.'

'Thank you very much.' She nodded and smiled, relieved.

'You must watch your road signs, miss, or you'll be in trouble. Be careful next time.' The policeman stood back and she turned in the direction he had given her.

'Phew!' breathed Dean. 'Thought our number was up. Thank heaven for whiskers. At least they hid my terror.'

'How do you suppose *I* felt?' sighed Pauline. 'The sooner we get to Bruce the better I'll be.'

On the outskirts of Hampstead Heath they booked at a small commercial hotel, left their bags and went on again in search of Bruce Dunn. 'Wish I could have left this hot-face decoration behind in my bag,' said Dean, rubbing the whiskers.

'You'll have to get used to them, it's your last chance. And now — here we are — this looks like the place.'

A genteel board informed them that this was 'Morston Rest Home', gold lettering on black. It appeared to be two strongly-built large grey houses made into one. Royal blue curtains at the broad windows, a few people sitting in sunny window bays, a lamp in front of the glass porch above three shallow steps. A sweeping drive led to the steps and a few bushes in tubs. If there were any gardens to the place they must be at the back of the premises.

'Do I wait here?' asked Dean. 'What

do you think?' Now about to meet people he felt vulnerable despite his ugly disguises, aware of the test just ahead of him.

'No, come along and get the first step over. You'd better start to mix with the public. It has to be faced, Dean. Just be natural. I'll help you up the steps as though you can't see well.'

'That's true enough. Everything is in a grey world with these specs.'

In the cool shaded hall Pauline went towards the curved front of the receptionist's desk. 'Is it possible to visit Mr Dunn, please? I know we should really come tomorrow, but we can't manage to get here then.' As the woman's keen eyes passed over Pauline's curly brown head and her neatly dressed figure, light coat over a soft floral dress — and then to her rather rough-looking companion, she added, 'We are friends of his — of his wrestling days.'

'I'll phone him.' The woman picked

up the cream-coloured telephone. 'Name, please.'

'Mrs Crompton. He might not remember my name.'

'Oh yes. Someone phoned for you yesterday.'

Pauline nodded. 'Yes. Mr Dunn said I could call on him. I had planned tomorrow but something came up —'

The woman spoke softly into the telephone. Pauline noticed now a name brooch on her lapel. 'Miss Soper.' She was an efficient young woman, younger than Pauline certainly, with straight auburn hair to the lobes of her ears and a fringe, and a very pale skin. She hung up and turned back to Pauline. 'Yes, you are to go over straight away.' At last she smiled. 'He sounds quite excited. He hasn't had many visitors. Go through that door, turn right and up the stairs. Room number six.'

'Thank you, Miss Soper,' said Pauline, and the woman smiled again. It probably made her day, thought Pauline, amused. Life here was no doubt a bit dreary.

At the top of the stairs a long polished wood floor with a grey runner carpet the whole length, one or two grey cushioned seats. They went past closed doors to No. 6. 'Must cost the earth here,' whispered Dean. 'But Bruce can take it.'

'Wait here, Dean,' said Pauline softly. 'Till I see how the land lies.'

'Sure. This rig-out of mine might give him a shock. Can't risk that.' He sank down on the seat nearby and she knocked on the door. A deep voice bade her enter. It was a pleasant room, catching the afternoon sun, overlooking some gardens. The window was pushed halfway up and the smell of new-mown grass wafted in. The man who was standing and holding out his hand was not unlike Dean's build, but his hair was fair and a few freckles were scattered about his pink round face. Brown eyes studied her face closely.

'Good afternoon,' said Bruce Dunn,

as they shook hands. 'I'm surprised they let you come up on non-visiting day, but possibly they waived the rules for once. They've been anxious, I think, because no one called to see me.' His gaze deepened. 'I'm very sorry but I can't remember you. It's regrettable, but I've been in a blank spot for so long — '

'It isn't your fault, Mr Dunn. We haven't met before. I've come to see you about an old friend of yours. Tell me, please, can you remember Dean Jameson?'

His face brightened, his full mouth widening into a smile. 'Of course, Dean, my mate. How is he? I wondered why he didn't come — where he had cleared off to. It hurt that he never tried to look me up. Sit down, Miss — er — '

'Call me Pauline as Dean does.' She still stood with her hand on the back of a chair. 'First, can you tell me the last time you saw Dean?' She held her breath while he pondered. This meant so much to her, to confirm all that Dean had told her.

'What has happened to him? We were wrestlers, you know. Is he ill? What's the matter?' His brow wrinkled. 'It was our last show — before I set off for Carlisle — the car crash.' He smiled wryly. 'You see I'm remembering things now. I'm not doing badly, am I?'

'I'm pleased you are doing so well, and more so that you might be able to help us. When did you last see Dean? Did you leave him at the wrestling ring?'

'There's something the matter,' he said anxiously. 'What has happened to him?'

'Just try to remember where you left him last. It's important for me to know, Mr Dunn. I'll tell you why later. Where did you leave him after the wrestling bouts that day?'

'Why, we went back to our digs together, of course. Good old Mrs Burley's — I only remembered her name the other day. Must write to her. Goodness knows what rubbish I left behind there. Yes, she used to call us inseparable. We went back to the digs to pack. I was going to Carlisle and Dean back home for a time. It was unusual for us not to be wrestling together in Carlisle, but it wasn't a tag match and Dean — I think his mother wasn't very well so he took the chance to go home — '

Pauline sighed happily. 'That is marvellous news. I have Dean here with me — waiting out in the passage — would you like to see him?'

Bruce sprang forward. '*Would* I like to see him! It will put new life into me.'

'Just a minute — you'll find him different. He has been in trouble and he's had to disguise himself — we'll explain all that later.' She reached the door ahead of Bruce and beckoned to Dean to come in.

'Dean — no!' Bruce gasped, astounded as his be-whiskered friend came near. 'You said — we always said, always clean-cut, no beards, long hair — ' He fingered Dean's rough whiskers. 'We weren't going to look like Jollop and some of them.'

'It comes off, all fake — ' laughed Dean, tossing off the cap and wig.

'A joke, eh? Not fair after so long — '

'I told you, it's a disguise,' put in Pauline. 'We had to do it to get here to see you. He has a lot to tell you.'

'It's great to see you again, anyway.' Bruce grasped the other man's shoulders. 'I lost you. Didn't know where you were, nobody would tell me anything.' He thumped Dean's chest. 'Still fighting fit, eh?'

'Our wrestling days are over, Bruce,' said Dean solemnly.

'Mine, yes — '

'Me, too. I've had enough. Now, listen, I want your help, Bruce. I'm in trouble, and only you can help me. It's a long story.'

'He remembers everything, Dean,' said Pauline. 'He will get you out of all this.'

She went over to the window and sat down, leaving them to it. They talked hard, Dean telling Bruce everything from the beginning of it all and what he had gone through. Bruce exclaiming in anger and disgust at times, distressed that he had been miles away and useless to help.

'My dear chap, what a thing to happen! To think you of all people — ' he shook his fair head. 'They won't let me watch wrestling — no one would tell me anything. I've had to keep quiet, to let my brain get into order.'

'You're back to normal now, though, aren't you?' said Dean anxiously. 'They'll accept anything you say as truth?'

'Oh yes, of course. My doctors know and Longford my solicitor — ' He struck his hands together. 'Longford. That's who we must have now. He'll sort all this out for you. There's no time to waste.'

Impulsively he jumped up, went to

his telephone and dialled a number. Dean smiled at Pauline, already visibly relaxed. Apparently a secretary answered the telephone. 'Bruce Dunn here. Will you put me through to Mr Longford, please.' As she must have hesitated — 'It's urgent. Please get him, he won't mind.' Bruce looked back at Dean as he waited and grinned. 'I'll be glad to see you without that fungus on your face. You look scruffy.'

'Sorry, Bruce. I'll try not to let anyone around here see me — if you only knew the trouble we've had — '

'I can guess that. You took a great risk. Lucky for you you dropped in on Pauline.'

'She's an angel.'

Pauline smiled. 'He doesn't really know me, does he? Who wouldn't have helped him — at least given him food and money?'

'Any other girl would have screamed blue murder,' said Dean.

'I had Rex to protect me,' chuckled Pauline.

Dean laughed. 'You can say that again.'

'And a mythical husband.'

Bruce's gaze sharpened. 'You're married? Oh yes, of course, Mrs Crompton — but it hadn't sunk in, I'm afraid.'

'I *was*. We quarrelled over wrestling more often than not. You won't know him, but Tony Crompton is your biggest fan, Bruce Dunn.'

Bruce turned away quickly and spoke into the telephone. 'Hello, Mr Longford. Bruce here. I must see you as soon as possible. Can you get over tomorrow? . . . No, it's terribly urgent and being Wednesday tomorrow . . . I want your help with something. Try and make it tomorrow, will you? It's something — I can't waste time, and I can't explain over the phone. It's a long story . . . You will, tomorrow afternoon. Thank you immensely. That's fine.' Bruce said goodbye and hung up.

13

Bruce turned back to Dean with clasped hands. 'We're on the way now, Dean boy. Longford will sort it all out for us.' He paused at a light knock on the door. A young man in a white hospital coat entered with afternoon tea on a tray.

'The tea you ordered, Mr Dunn.'

'Thank you, Riley. Very good of you, especially as it's not visiting day.'

The man smiled. 'Being as it's you, Mr Dunn. I've just seen Doctor Lamb and he's pleased for you to have some company at last.'

'Yes,' said Bruce, as the door closed behind the man. 'It's something to do with rehabilitating me. It's been a bit boring and dull, long hours by myself. They've all tried hard, coming in at odd times and trying to get me interested in things, but I've felt deserted. When I came round you were the first person I thought of, Dean. Couldn't understand why you didn't care enough to ask how I was.'

'Even if I'd known I couldn't have got to you.'

'No. We've both had a raw deal, but it will soon be over now.' Bruce clapped his big hands together. 'We'll have a new start. What are you thinking of doing? Will you pour the tea, Pauline?' He passed the plate of sandwiches to Dean.

'I can't tell you all I have in mind,' said Dean, glancing at Pauline; 'but you remember how I always hankered after an open-air life, how my happiest hours were at home helping Dad on the land — '

'You're going back to help him — '

'No. He's got a good man and a young lad working there now, so he isn't overworked. No, I'll be looking for a place of my own, a smallholding in the South somewhere.' He glanced at Pauline again. Her colour had deepened as she listened. So he meant to stay near to her, she thought . . .

'Well, it sounds great. Maybe I can come and help, eh?' said Bruce eagerly.

'Let's not jump ahead, Bruce. Let me feel free and safe first. I hardly dare hope — now it's going to come out in the open — '

'It will be all right. Your worries will soon be over. Come tomorrow and meet Mr Longford. Be sure to come. He's a busy man and I daren't waste his time.'

'I'll be here, you can be sure of that,' said Dean confidently.

'He'll be here at two sharp, so if you can come about three o'clock it will give me chance to explain everything first. You won't be such a shock to him.'

'That will suit me fine. Three o'clock,' agreed Dean, fingering his bushy beard.

'And keep that disguise on till we've set things in motion. I don't want you picked up by the police at the eleventh hour. It would delay everything.'

'I *am* an escaped convict — ' said Dean ruefully.

'Don't call yourself such names,' said Pauline.

'If you hadn't got out you would never have found me or proved your innocence,' said Bruce. 'It will all work out, Dean. Just be cautious for a while.'

'Somewhere there's a murderer walking about free,' the thought suddenly struck Pauline.

Bruce nodded. 'Yes, and in a way I wish him luck. Vincent asked to be bumped off. He had no friends — a vicious character.'

'He shouldn't have been in the wrestling ring,' said Dean. 'However tough we get it is sport, after all.'

'Have some more cake, Pauline,' said Bruce, as she rose and picked up her light coat.

'I've had quite enough, thank you, and the tea was really welcome. I felt so dry with the warmth — and excitement as well, I expect. You won't need me any more, will you?' she said. 'No need for me to come tomorrow?'

'No, dear, you can leave the lad to me now. He'll be in safe hands.'

'So I'll drop him here at three tomorrow, then go back home. All right, Dean?'

He smiled wryly. 'I'll be sorry to lose you, but you've done all you can, Pauline. It's up to Bruce now to proclaim my innocence to the world.'

'And Mr Longford.' Bruce stood up, testing his lame leg carefully. 'Well, time is getting on so I'll let you be on your way.' He held out his hand to Pauline. 'Many thanks for bringing my old chum back, Pauline. I agree with him, you are an angel.'

Dean donned his wig and cap and they left soon afterwards, fortunately seeing no one but the receptionist again on the way out. It was a quiet, peaceful place. No doubt several patients spent the afternoons resting. Dean looked relieved as they reached the car, then gasped as he sat down. 'Cripes, this seat is blazing hot!'

Pauline laughed. 'Yes, it's stifling in here, isn't it? I think Summer has come for a while. We should have parked somewhere shady.'

'You've no idea — I feel like a stuffed potato under all this hairy stuff.'

'You'll soon be free of it, I hope. You've forgotten the glasses. You've a good excuse for wearing them this sunny day.'

'Have a heart, Pauline. I'm hot enough without any more furniture on my face.' As they drew up to their small hotel, he said, 'I suppose I'd better get back to my room and keep under cover — '

'Yes, put your feet up and have a rest. I'm off to do some shopping but I won't be long.'

'Pauline, can't we have a night out? Let's go somewhere.'

'Really, Dean — what a risk!' She looked him over anxiously.

'We could have a meal out, in one of those dark, candlelit places and a second show somewhere. I'll trim myself up. Plenty of lads with beards nowadays — who's going to notice one quiet chap?'

'We'll see later on. I won't be long away, Dean, I feel like a rest myself after our short night. I somehow think gallivanting will be off this evening.'

'Well, maybe.' He yawned, remembering their hours of driving and dawdling till they could call on Bruce. 'It's selfish of me to think of it. You've had a hard day, Pauline.'

'When we've had a rest, wash and brush-up, we'll feel different, no doubt, so we'll make no plans till later on. That suit you?'

'Yes, fine.' He yawned again. 'See you later.'

Pauline parked the car, took the tube up to the city and enjoyed an hour or so looking round the big stores, and buying a few articles she had been wanting, her tiredness wearing off with her new interests. When she got back to the hotel there was no sight nor sound of Dean in the room next to hers. She took off her dress and shoes, dropped on the bed, pulled up the eiderdown and instantly fell asleep. It was almost eleven before she started awake again. And Dean had wanted to go places, she thought uneasily. She hurriedly washed and dressed and went to Dean's door.

She knocked gently. 'Dean, are you awake?'

There was no response so she tried the handle. The door opened and she peeped in. He was sound asleep, only the top of his dark head showing above the bed-clothes. All his exhaustion and days of worry had caught up with him at last. His clothes were strewn about the room, lying where he had dropped them off wearily, and she smiled at the wig crowned with the cap on the knob of a chair back. It was a shame to disturb him. She crept out and pondered what to do. Here was an end, indeed, to their evening plans. She was feeling hungry and guessed Dean would be when he awoke. It was perhaps still possible to get sandwiches in the hotel. If not there was a chip shop not far away.

There was quite a lot of life going on in the hotel she found when she went downstairs, plenty of chatter and noise even though the bar was no doubt closed by now, and there were a few men having a late meal in the panelled dining-room. The management were only too pleased to provide her with supper, and said they would bring it up to her room at once. She decided against a hot meal, not wanting to disturb Dean, and made a choice of sausage rolls, ham sandwiches, doughnuts and a pot of hot coffee.

'We'll probably have indigestion after this so late at night,' she laughed; 'but it's quite a while since we had something to eat.' They had been so busy talking with Bruce that they had eaten little of the tea provided there.

'Better than being hungry, anyway,' joked the young waiter. 'Even that keeps me awake. We've got indigestion tablets if you need 'em.'

That didn't sound so complimentary to their food, thought Pauline with amusement, as she wandered back to her room. The waiter followed soon after and put the tray of food on the little writing-table.

'If there's anything else — any time — just ring,' he said, indicating the bell button near the bed. 'There's always someone on call.'

She thanked and tipped him lavishly, so pleased to be served so well and for his good humour. What a pity they had left the flask in the car, she thought, it would have kept the coffee hot for Dean. She wrapped a towel about the coffee-pot and hoped for the best. Luckily she hadn't to wait long. About ten minutes later Dean was knocking at her door. 'Pauline — '

'Come in.'

He entered, his clothes dragged on and his hair standing on end. 'Pauline, I'm so sorry. Why didn't you wake me? The evening has gone west.'

‘It doesn’t matter. Sit down and eat. This is now your evening meal. If the coffee is too cold by now, I’ll send for more.’

‘You think of everything. I feel ravenous.’ He picked up a sandwich and took a big bite. ‘I’ve let you down, Pauline, after all my high-and-mighty talk.’

‘I don’t think either of us was up to much this evening. It’s reaction, I expect, the release from our anxieties.’

‘We’re always having midnight feasts, aren’t we? Can’t say I don’t enjoy them, all the same.’

‘There’s plenty of time ahead of us. We’ll have a celebration outing when this business is all cleared up.’

He laid a hand over hers. ‘You do believe I’ll come through all right, don’t you?’

‘Of course I do. You can’t possibly give up hope now.’

‘As you say, it’s reaction after being so tensed up, always on the watch, hiding from everyone — now suddenly to be walking about, nearing the climax.' He smiled uncertainly. 'There's all the police and legal part of it to face now.'

'With Bruce and his good solicitor behind you, you can't fail now. I'm sure it will be easier than you think. They won't want to make a song and dance of it after such a drastic mistake.'

'You're such a help. I couldn't have done it without you.' Dean sighed. 'Must you go back tomorrow, Pauline?'

She smiled and nodded. 'I'd only be in the way now. It's up to you and Bruce.'

They emptied the plates and drank the coffee and went on talking over the day's events. In the early hours Dean rose reluctantly and went back to his room. The following morning they went for a drive, to keep Dean relaxed and rested before his important meeting with Mr Longford, and they had lunch at a small country inn. Dean had trimmed the beard and wig and smoothed them down with some lotion Bruce had persisted on him using. Prompt on three o'clock Pauline dropped him at the Morston Rest Home. He waited a moment at the open window beside her.

'Wish me luck, Pauline.'

She smiled. 'I think Luck is on your side at last, Dean.'

'Thank you for everything, love, especially for your belief in me.' He bent and pressed his lips to her warm cheek. 'Wait at the cottage for me. I'll be back.'

'Make it as soon as you can.' Wistfully she watched him go up the steps, look back and wave, then go inside. She turned the car out of the gateway and set off in the direction of home. She felt lost without him and wished she at least had Rex sitting beside her. Now they had achieved their object, and in spite of definite hope for him, she felt in low spirits. She had time to dwell on her own feelings now. He said he would be back, but would he? With Bruce again, once cleared and free, perhaps his old life would come crowding about him again. He might have second thoughts about starting his smallholding. She would just be in the background, a mere instrument towards his freedom. She knew now that she needed him, wanted him desperately.

She had never felt like this about Tony. Even after her anger over him and Teresa, and he had left her, there was no aching emptiness like this. They had been playmates, inexperienced, there had been no passion or deep feeling between them, they even found how greatly their interests differed. He was all outdoor sport, lively parties and pretty girls that he cast aside as soon as boredom set in. She only needed her books and art, her drawing-board holding her more and more enslaved. Vanessa's cute little characters amused and took hold of her, the chance of illustrating them couldn't be denied, and from this other work had come along. She had soon settled into a life without Tony. She hardly blamed him, her anger had been chiefly against Teresa, especially for her unkindness towards their parents, and Tony could be so charming and penitent when he chose. Now Dean — if he let her down, his promises mere fluffy thoughts — this time her heart would break. Nothing would ever be the same again.

14

Busy with her thoughts and it being early closing day in many towns, Pauline reached her own village much quicker than expected. As though to match her gloomy thoughts the sky was lowering now, and it had been raining for the last hour or so. She slowed up near Theo's cottage but there was no one about, so she went on, deciding to collect Rex after she had opened up her own place, and perhaps this sharp shower of rain would have ceased. Just as well she hadn't lingered, too, she found, coming across a familiar little red car on the grass verge outside Lilac Cottage. Vanessa, a raincape thrown over her head, was still knocking on the door with evident impatience.

'Where the devil have you been?' she demanded, as Pauline ran up the path to join her. 'I've been hanging about the village, had a meal at the pub. This is my third trip to your door. You never warned me.'

'Sorry, Vanessa. I've been up to London.'

'London! Can't you survive without city life, after all? Or maybe another publisher — ' hinted Vanessa, shaking her raincape as they went indoors regardless of furniture.

'No, you and Harmon-Richleys keep me busy enough.'

'Well, you don't depend on us, either, do you? It's more of a hobby with you.'

'The parents left me quite comfortably off, yes, but you know I can't resist drawing-paper and paints.'

'Well, then — what's the mystery?' persisted Vanessa. 'You never said you were going away. You haven't been here two minutes.'

How possessive Vanessa could be sometimes! thought Pauline. 'It was something urgent that turned up. I had to go — something unexpected.'

‘Ah-ha!’ Vanessa wagged a finger at her. ‘There’s a man in the case, isn’t there? Why make a mystery of it? I saw your Mrs Thingammy who cleans and she said you’d had a man here. That you called him cousin, but I don’t believe that any more than she does.’

Mrs Elton, that interfering little sharp-nosed creature! thought Pauline furiously. ‘Why doesn’t she mind her own business! And you, too, Vanessa Dorne!’

‘Oh come, Pauline, pals and all that. You know I’ve been anxious for you to find another mate. You’re not like me — fellows to me are a nuisance except on business — but you need someone to fill that silly Tony’s place, you know you do. If I’m going to hear wedding bells again you know I’ll be delighted for you — it’s not just nosiness.’

‘Sorry, Vanessa, for being uppity, but I’m beginning to feel it will be necessary to shake Mrs Elton off — if that’s at all possible. Yes, there is someone, but I can’t tell you all about it till this business in London is settled. Then I hope we'll be free to talk.'

'You're in love! I thought there was something different about you, a sort of glow or something. What's holding you up? Don't tell me the fellow is waiting for a divorce or some such thing.'

'No, he's not been married before. It's simply business that we have to keep quiet for the moment. Then I hope — ' Pauline's thoughts fled back to Dean and she wondered how his day had gone.

'Then a wedding. Bless you, love. It *must* go well for you this time. Now, look, I want you to read through this.' With her usual abruptness the subject was changed and Vanessa unwrapped a packet and took out a thick wad of carbon typed papers. 'It's that story for older children you suggested. Twins, boy and girl, and a younger sister, I'll have to call them the Terrible Three or something. See what you think of it, and if it's worthwhile do some illustrations. Myself I think it's rather funny, but who am I to judge?'

'How interesting.' Pauline turned over the first page or two of the carbon copy. 'I'll enjoy reading it, and it will fill my time while I'm waiting for news from London.'

'At least you're encouraging.' Vanessa, sprawled on the settee, looked about her. 'There's something missing here — where's the pup?'

'I had to leave him down at Moor Cottage for a day or two. I'm going down for him soon. What would you like, Vanessa? Tea? There might be some cake in the tin.'

'Tea, certainly. I'm terribly dry — that cook at the pub has a heavy hand with the salt. You know, Pauline' — Vanessa called after her as Pauline went down to the rear quarters — 'I thought for a time that you and that chappie at the cottage below were going to get together.'

'He's a sweet man, and we're marvellous friends,' replied Pauline, reappearing with crockery on a tray.

'But, in spite of everything he is still devoted to that unfaithful wife of his.'

'She doesn't deserve it. Some women get away with murder,' murmured Vanessa. In spite of her intense curiosity, she did not refer to Pauline's London visit again, and they talked of various other things before she rose to go. 'Oh, I forgot to tell you,' she said, pulling on her tweed jacket, 'I saw your late husband the other night — a house-warming party. Surrounded by adoring girls as usual. You're well rid of him, I guess, Pauline.'

'Did you speak to him?' asked Pauline anxiously.

'Of course not. I don't think he knows me. Anyway, he wouldn't notice me. I wouldn't fit into his beauty chorus.'

'He's not so bad, he has his good points, and he can't help being so confoundedly handsome,' returned Pauline with relief. Vanessa might have heard more news of Pauline's new 'lover' if she had made herself known to Tony.

'Don't make excuses for him. He wasn't true to you and never would have been. You ask for trouble.'

'Maybe.' Pauline smiled, remembering her welcome of a stranger who had escaped from the jail across the moors. That could have been trouble, too, certainly; but he looked so wretched and ill, wet through and hobbling on one leg — and there had been something — unexplainable — between them from the start . . .

'What are you dreaming about?' Vanessa smiled down into her eyes. 'All right — I won't ask.' She went over to the door. 'So long, Pauline. I'm hoping to hear some good news of you next time. I do miss that pup. He seemed to bring something to the place, gave it a homely finish.' Laughing she went off, and a few minutes later the horrible little car clattered away.

Pauline read a few pages of the new children's story then suddenly pushed it away. Vanessa was right, the cottage wasn't the same without Rex padding around or dreaming in his corner. She'd go down and fetch him at once. Dusk was falling and it was colder than of late, but it had stopped raining for a time. She had no chance to say a word to Theo as the dog ran rings around her, leaping and nearly bowling her over in his exuberance, with little grunts of delight, so relieved to have her back.

Theo Gale was laughing. 'I believe he thought he'd really lost you this time.'

'Poor old Rex. Down, lad, you're too big and strong. I hope he hasn't been a trouble.'

'Of course not, but you can tell he must have been inwardly fretting. He'll understand better another time.'

'I hope so, in case I have to be away any time again.'

'Are you coming in for a while?'

'Isn't Brenda here?'

'No, and I'm missing her. Her

mother is ill so she has gone to her. Come in, Pauline.'

'Just a short time, then. I haven't been home long.' Feeling that he needed company she went in, the dogs pushing against her affectonately, and into his living-room. Theo followed and closed the door. 'What is the matter with Brenda's mother? Nothing serious, I hope.'

'No, I don't think so, but I can't get to the bottom of it. Just low spirits, depression it seems. I wish I could do something, but I might only make things worse. Brenda, with her big cheerful heart, is the best companion for her, I'm sure. Now, how have you gone on, Pauline? Are your affairs working out well?'

'Over the worst now, I hope.' Pauline hesitated, then deciding though for some reason she couldn't confide in Vanessa it was different with Theo, so she went on, 'I think I can tell you at last, Theo, as it must be out in the open by now and can't hurt — him.

You'll think me an idiot and I can't explain how or why it happened this way, I just felt compelled to go along with it. It all started with the man who escaped from the jail, do you remember?'

'Of course, but we haven't heard of him again. Dangerous Dean.'

'He's not dangerous, Theo, that was just a sort of showman's name, he's — he's delightful.' Pauline laughed. 'That's funny, a new name for him, Delightful Dean. Theo, he is the man you all heard of and saw in my cottage — my gardener, my cousin. The man I am madly in love with.'

'For heaven's sake, Pauline, no! Whatever are you talking about?'

'Listen, it's quite a story.' She told him word for word how Dean had limped into her shed to hide and Rex discovered him, how she had given him shelter, and then all their difficulties that followed.

'Pauline, whatever made you do it? He could have been really bad, you could have been murdered — '

'It was a mad thing to do, I suppose, but I seemed to know there was nothing bad about him. It's hard to explain — I think we both fell in love at first sight. Rex liked him — '

'That stupid pup — '

'Never mind, he helped to guard me in his way. I've more to tell you, Theo. Dean is a good man and has been wrongly treated. He is with friends at last, busy proving his innocence.'

When the whole story was told Theo sat in silence for a moment with clasped hands. Then he said quietly, 'It must be a vast relief to you both now that he has found his friend, the only proof he had. But you, Pauline, what about you? You've let your heart rule your head, haven't you?'

'I hope — I'm sure we'll get together in the end. He has told me to wait here for him.'

'I don't want you to be hurt again. Supposing — it's just that he knew he was on a good way out with you — '

'I'm going to work hard and try not to think of him too much. But I'm sure he'll come — we are meant for each other. I feel so sure.'

'There's nothing I can say, is there? Only that I want you to be happy. I hope you will find true happiness at last. I'm a helpless sort of fellow, but if there is ever anything I can do — '

'You are a great comfort, Theo.' She laid a hand over his. 'It's been a relief to tell you about it. I have been so tensed up lately and we daren't confide in anyone. If you had known you would have been anxious for everybody's sake, probably believing I was threatened in some way. You might have got the police for my safety — '

'I can't say how I would have reacted, it's such a remarkable story. I probably wouldn't have believed him innocent. We have both known unhappiness, unfaithfulness — are you perfectly sure he — this man — isn't just a rebound, a second-best — '

'It's the true thing this time. I've

never felt like this before, and even if — if he doesn't come, I'll be glad I met him and helped him.'

'Good for you, Pauline. If only — ' Theo stopped and sighed. 'No, I won't think back, that's over, we have to go on. How about getting us a drink of coffee before you leave? Or something stronger? You must be dry after all that talking.'

'Oh, coffee please, Theo, I'd love some. Put a record on while I get it.'

She went across to the kitchen that was almost as big as the other room, Rex at her heels, determined not to let her get away from him this time. While she got the supper mugs that Theo found more convenient to hold and prepared the coffee, strains of Chopin's lighter music drifted across the little hall. With it her spirits lifted again. She mustn't start fretting for Dean. It was all in the lap of the gods, as they said. Humming to the well-known music she carried the hot coffee to Theo. His face was peaceful now as he listened, his eyes closed, music always a solace to him, and he had for years had great need of it, she knew.

'I'll have to be going, Theo,' she said, as they drank the coffee. 'I haven't done a thing at the cottage, not even unpacked my bag. Besides,' she laughed, 'if Mrs Elton knew anything about this I'd be at least the scarlet woman she thinks me.'

'Don't worry, Pauline. At heart she is quite fond of you. Bonny and I will walk up the road with you.'

'That would be nice. I don't think it's raining now.'

A few minutes later they set off. It was fine but water trickled in the ditches and the sky was heavy and dark. Bonny cleverly guided her master around the few puddles. 'Feels like rain again,' said Theo, lifting his face to the cool, damp air.

'It looks like it, too,' said Pauline. 'Not a star in sight. Here we are. You're not going any further, are you?'

'I'll just let Bonny have a run on the moor at the top then go back. You go in now, Pauline, and get some rest, and promise me' — his hand felt for her arm and held it — 'no more escaped prisoners. If one escapes never do it again — bolt the doors.'

She laughed. 'I promise faithfully. Only now do I realize what a mad thing it was to do, but however long I try I'll never find an explanation for it. It was something beyond myself.'

He went on his way, evidently believing that she had come out of this escapade so luckily, and that she would never let it happen again. While Rex explored every corner of the cottage to make sure it was as he had left it, she cleared out the picnic basket and unpacked her small suitcase. She pictured Dean back in his hotel room, perhaps happier and more relieved than he had been for a very long time. All that there was left for her to do now was wait and hope — for both of them . . .

15

A week passed, then another, and Pauline found herself worrying. Why didn't Dean phone? Of course he wanted to feel sure of everything before getting in touch with her again, but just to hear his voice would have eased her mind. Surely it couldn't go wrong now! She tried to bury herself in Vanessa's book and make plans for illustrations — the book was certainly amusing and intriguing, no doubt about that — but she would find her mind wandering. She would get up to gaze out at the empty moors on one side, or the silent road from the windows on the other side. This usually resulted in Rex getting up and waiting expectantly by the door, and his tail would wag furiously as she nearly always said, 'All right, come along, Rex, let's go for a walk.'

Whatever the weather they had at least one daily ramble, exploring the rises and dips of the moors, with its ever-changing colours of gorse bushes, fern patches and heather clumps, and mossy outcrops of rock. It would have been a bad time without her affectionate, playful dog, and yet so short a while ago she had searched for weeks for a suitable lonely cottage, where she could find solitude and do her work in peaceful quietness. Yet she had enjoyed Dean's companionship, realizing at last that two people *could* live in harmony and trust each other.

She had returned from one of these leisurely walks one day when she saw Brenda Gale coming up the lane. Rex leapt forward eagerly to greet the girl and Pauline followed.

'Hello, Brenda. I'm glad to see you back again. Your father missed you. How is your mother?'

'Getting better, she'll be all right now.' Brenda's face glowed, she looked radiant with happiness. 'She's here. She came home with me. Pauline, I've got them together again.'

'Oh, Brenda, how marvellous! You did it,' said Pauline, with delight. 'I'm so relieved for your father.'

'Yes, he's like a new man. I want you to come to meet Mother, Pauline. Come now.'

'Yes, I will. This is too good to miss.'

As they turned about to go down the lane, Brenda said, 'She's lost weight and she's rather quiet, but it's nothing serious. She'll pick up now, I know she needed Dad just as much as he needed her. I told a few white lies, of course — I told her Dad knew she was ill and if she didn't come home he was coming to fetch her. And, Pauline — ' she looked up shyly — 'I laid it on a bit about you being around, and I think that really geared her into action.' She laughed. 'She must love him to be jealous.'

'Oh, Brenda — '

'She'll like you, though. I'm sorry, I

hope you don't really mind. It doesn't matter now she's home and knows Dad wants her so much.'

'I'll forgive you,' laughed Pauline. 'I would have tried anything to get her back, as I know life means little to Theo without her. He'd have gone under if it hadn't been for you, Brenda.'

They reached Moor Cottage and went inside. Immediately Pauline sensed there was something different. It was in the air, an attractive scented atmosphere. 'That's Mother's French perfume,' said Brenda, seeing the other's face lifted as she breathed in the air. 'She's a terror for that expensive stuff, rather have it than new clothes. I expect she's been having a bath.'

Pauline went into the living-room, while the girl disappeared in the back regions. Theo came forward holding out his hands, smiling. His face was younger, happier. Pauline caught at his hands. 'Theo, I can't say how glad I am. This is how it should be, all of you together.'

'Isn't it wonderful! I hardly dared hope it could ever happen, although we had been so close before. I tried to adjust to living alone — '

'You've been so courageous on your own, Theo. You deserve this new chance of happiness.'

'A new chance, yes. I hope I can keep her now, Pauline, that she doesn't find me a burden.'

'You are as good as any man, there isn't much you are unable to do. Your wife must realize that now, and the other world she tried — she has found it wanting. Don't let it worry you, it won't happen again.'

'Here they are now — ' he murmured, and a moment later Brenda led her mother into the room. Valerie Gale was still as beautiful as her photograph, but she was slimmer and a little pale. She looked elegant in a blue and gold kaftan, banded at her wrists and up to her little chin. Her dark hair was built high and some short strands still curled damply about her forehead after her hot bath. Pauline wished so much that Theo could see her.

'So this is Pauline,' she said, in her light merry voice. 'I've heard a lot about you.'

'And I have of you,' said Pauline, shaking her small slim hand. 'It's lovely to see you at last.'

'Thank you for keeping an eye on Theo for me.'

'I think it's more the other way round, Theo helping me. I haven't been here so long, you know.'

'I hope you'll stay,' said Valerie. 'It will be nice to have you still popping in to see us, and I believe you do some typing for Theo.'

'I love the cottage,' said Pauline; 'and I have no plans for ever leaving — ' but even as she spoke she thought of Dean. Where did he hope to settle?

'You'll stay for tea, won't you? Brenda is a dab hand at cakemaking, and I know there is one ready waiting.'

Pauline agreed, she was eager to

know more of this wayward, repentant, lively woman. The two dogs had settled down contentedly together, and Theo had come close to his wife, his arm about her shoulders.

'She's been neglecting herself,' he said fondly, 'and now we are going to give her a lot of care. I don't know why she didn't come home before, feeling so depressed and ill.'

As Pauline helped to wash up later, Valerie said quietly, 'I feel so awful leaving Theo like I did. I can't think what possessed me. It turned out all such a wash-out, too. However could I think that giddy life with — with anyone else could replace Theo. I think I was shocked, scared of the thought of taking on the responsibility of a sightless man. I didn't know how clever, how independent he could be. I'm ashamed, Pauline. I don't know how to make it up to him.'

'Just being here, back home with him is all he wants. Simply be happy in each other's company as you were before.'

'You know I have a feeling that we could go about together a bit as we did before,' mused Valerie, pleating the tea-towel as she dreamed. 'A holiday, somewhere where Bonny could go, somewhere that Theo knows. He could picture it all again as I talk to him.'

'Suggest it to him. It might be refreshing for both of you, and no doubt help him with his travel articles.'

After leaving the happy trio at Moor Cottage, Pauline found her own cottage seemed even more deadly quiet and lonely. 'I'll really have to shake myself out of this,' she said to Rex, as he watched with his silken head tipped to one side inquisitively, because there was no one else to talk to. 'Getting moody like this is hopeless . . . ' Well, there was always work. She stooped over the coloured pictures scattered about the table. The ginger-haired, freckled twins and their mischievous curly-headed younger sister. She was getting involved with them almost as much as with Vanessa's comical characters, Muffit and Mopsie. When the telephone rang she almost jumped out of her skin.

'Hello, Pauline Crompton,' she said, not expecting anyone in particular.

'Hello, darling!'

'Darling! Who's that?'

A well-known chuckle at the other end. 'How many men call you darling, then? It's Dean here, of course.'

'Oh, Dean, at last!' She sighed with relief. 'How are you?'

'Fine. All's going well, Pauline. I'm walking about a free man without whiskers, too, but I have to hang around till they've fiddled and fixed everything up. It's started a real hooha here. They've been mixing with the wrestlers' lot, and they're even going into Vincent's private life — you know the chap who was killed. As I didn't do it, there must be someone who did. They've even been to see our old landlady, Mrs Burley.'

'Couldn't she have spoken for you before?'

'She wouldn't know if I was with Bruce or if I was, how long I stayed with him. She never knew where we were two minutes together. Popping in and out, often off to other towns.'

'You sound much happier, Dean.'

'I'm on top of the world. Bruce is searching thoroughly for a likely looking smallholding or plot of land for us both to work. I'll come as soon as I can, Pauline.'

'Make it soon. The place seems empty without you.'

'How is your friend Theo?'

'You can take that jealous tone out of your voice. His wife has come back to him.'

'Good for him. Glad to hear he's out of the running, because you're going to marry me, see?'

'Am I?'

'Of course, we both know that. I'll be there one day, but you understand about them wanting me on the spot yet, don't you?'

'Of course. We want it all cut and

dried and done with, then we can forget all about it.'

'I won't forget the day I took possession of your shed. Pauline — '

'Yes?' — as he hesitated.

'I love you,' he said, and the phone clicked off.

'Dean — ' but he had gone. His words still rang, glowing warmly, in her ears. 'I'll be there one day. I love you.' Greatly relieved and happy she returned to her sketching, but had no sooner picked up her pen than the telephone rang again. Dean with more to say?

But it was Vanessa with perfect timing, just as though she knew . . . 'Pauline, Vanessa here — I've just thought, when you get married again will you be leaving the cottage?'

Pauline almost lost her breath. 'I've no idea — never thought about it — and I'm not getting married yet. I want to keep the cottage if I can. I love it here.'

'Well, just thought about it. Give

me the first chance, won't you, if you decide to sell?'

'All right, but there's no chance of it yet, Vanessa. What about your new book? I like it immensely, should take with the kids. I've about finished illustrating, I think, if you want to come up and look them over.'

'I'll be along sometime. I'm into a new book, I'm already hooked on the Terrible Trio.'

'All right, be seeing you. Goodbye.'

'Pauline, any good news yet — of you?'

Pauline laughed. 'Everything is coming along fine. Nothing definite yet, though.'

'Well, hurry it up. Goodbye.'

Pauline hung up the receiver and stared dreamily at Rex. He promptly rolled over on his back, paws waving the air, ready for a fuss. She knelt down beside him and tickled his creamy-haired tummy. 'We don't want to leave here, do we, Rex? This has become a special place to us.' He bent his head and licked her hand.

The next few minutes would be his, he knew, for petting and play.

So the weeks passed. Why did legal matters have to take so long? thought Pauline. Dean was proved innocent and was quite free, but while they probed into everything it was easier for him to be on hand, instead of travelling backwards and forwards. Would he get any recompense, Pauline wondered, for all his ghastly time behind bars? Brenda and her mother had been up to Lilac Cottage once or twice, and they and Theo came to tea once. They all seemed very close and happy, a family again, more settled and affectionate since their separation. Theo and Valerie had been quietly married again, and it was all a topic for Mrs Elton for a while.

'It's lovely to see my poor Mr Gale so happy again, and so wonderful of him to take her back as though nothing had happened. Myself, I find it hard to forgive her. Leaving him blind, going off with another fellow, and a right rotter he turned out to be.'

'We'll have to forget all that, Mrs Elton,' said Pauline, trying to stem her chatter. 'All that matters is Mr Gale's happiness and Brenda's. She was foolish, carried away by a flashy young man, she knows it now and is truly ashamed and repentant. She will make it up to her husband now. She's really a nice woman.'

'Oh yes, she's nice enough and somehow I like her. But the way they go on, you'd think she had never left him like that.'

'It's turned out for the best, we ought to be pleased about that.'

'Yes, I suppose so, but I can never understand such women.' The woman turned suddenly and stared at Pauline. 'Are you going to get back with your husband, then?'

'No, Mrs Elton,' said Pauline, a little impatiently. 'That was all a stupid mistake from the start, and don't blame me — it wasn't my fault it petered out.'

'Eh no, I'm not thinking that, but I heard Mrs Gale say something about a marriage — '

'I think I'll be getting married again — to someone else — before long, that's probably what you heard.'

For once Mrs Elton was almost lost for her last word. 'Well, indeed — ' she said, but that was the end of it for the time being.

Her present illustrating work about finished, Pauline turned her attention to the garden. After a bit of tidying up in the front she strolled round to the back to look at the vegetables that were flourishing there from the seeds Dean had put in. She would have to be putting some cabbage plants and other greens in soon, she thought, or it was going to be too late. She was busy with the hoe in that back patch when a hand suddenly descended on her shoulder. With a quick Judo reflex she flung the person over her shoulder to the other side of the garden. Then she burst out laughing as she watched Dean Jameson disentangle himself from the clinging, thorny rambler by the wall. Rex came out of the shed where he had been rooting around old pots and sacks, and stood by barking excitedly.

'It's all right you laughing,' Dean protested, then getting free at last came up to her, rubbing scratched hands. 'That was some Judo throw, no idle boast on your part. I never really believed you.'

'Don't ever creep up on me again like that,' she said sternly. 'I'm sorry, Dean, but it just comes naturally, I never stopped to think.'

'I'll watch out next time, you can be sure of that, but now I'll get my own back.' His strong arms went round her, clamping her arms to her back, gripping her so tightly she could hardly breathe. A wrestler's bear-hug she realized, trying to struggle. His face came down to hers and as his hold slackened he pressed his lips hard to hers. 'Did I tell you I love you, darling Pauline?'

'Yes — you did,' she gasped.

'Will you marry me at once?'

'I thought you'd never ask.'

'Well, I had to get clear of all the mud first, come to you clean and unfettered — all right, Rex, I'm not hurting her — ' He kissed Pauline again then bent to caress the dog who was pushing urgently at his legs. 'I do believe he's jealous, but he'll have to share you with me from now on.'

'Come inside and tell me all you've been doing,' she said. 'You need a brush down and there's soil on your face and jacket.' Pauline held up her mud-stained hands.

'Never mind, it's all worth it. Kiss me again, Pauline — it's all too much like a dream yet. Sometimes I'm afraid I'll wake up still in that bleak old place.'

They went indoors, brushed and straightened themselves up then fell together on the settee. Rex, not to be outdone, rushed and laid across them, his front legs and chest over their knees.

'Well!' laughed Dean. 'How does one make love with a great big pooch holding us down?'

'He'll learn — ' began Pauline, and was silenced by Dean's urgent, long-suppressed kisses.

After a while they talked. 'Bruce has come up with a promising smallholding,' he told her. 'Only about twelve miles from here. Ideal. There are a few hens and pigs and plenty of ground and scope to build it up. You don't want to leave this cottage, do you?'

'I want to try and keep it, I like it so much.'

'So do I, so we won't leave it.'

'But won't the moors upset you — remembering?'

'No, we're actually several miles away from — that place, you know. If I get a little car the smallholding is quite convenient, and there's a cottage attached to it. Bruce suggests he lives there to keep an eye on things. It will make a new man of him. He will always be lame but he is too fine a man to go on lingering in that rest home. Even taking charge of me all these weeks has reawakened him.'

'It all sounds delightful, Dean.' Pauline's spirits rose. Not to leave her lovely cute little cottage and still have Dean — she couldn't have wished for more.

'So that's settled. I'll have a home, a wife and a job. By the way,' added Dean, remembering, 'the murderer has been found.'

'Oh dear.' Pauline didn't know whether to be relieved or sorry.

'We can't get at him, he's dead, committed suicide some time back. So I'm glad of that. He was a cousin of Vincent's and had been treated rottenly by him in some way. I can understand his feelings, knowing Vincent. He was a born trouble-maker.'

'I'm so glad it's all at an end now,' said Pauline.

'Yes, so that's that,' he said, drawing

her head back to his shoulder. 'Now we can make wedding plans.'

Much later Dean said, 'Will anybody be shocked if I stay here the night?'

Pauline laughed. 'I can only think of one, but I've got past caring what she thinks. *If* she gets to know it will be a new piece of gossip for her. You've spent plenty of nights here so why the sudden embarrassment?'

'It's different now, I'm no stranger. I don't trust myself — so lock your door, my love.'

'It means the camp bed again.'

'So what? I'm so tired I could sleep here now in your arms.'

As Dean was about to close his door that night he said, 'You know you did a dangerous thing taking a strange man into your house — and a so-called murderer at that.'

'I know,' said Pauline, 'but don't ask me to explain my madness. In some way I felt compelled. I took a great risk, I suppose, but somehow — I don't know why — I believed you,

Dean. I — er — fell for you right from the start.'

'Well, just don't let such a thing happen again.'

She smiled, recalling Theo's identical words. 'I won't, I promise you. You can be sure of that.'

'Till tomorrow, then. Good night, my love,' and the door closed.

Smiling, Pauline dropped into bed knowing that in a very short time, no door would ever be locked between them again. Dean was no stranger now. He was safe at home.

THE END

Other titles in the Linford Romance Library

SAVAGE PARADISE
Sheila Belshaw

For four years, Diana Hamilton had dreamed of returning to Luangwa Valley in Zambia. Now she was back — and, after a close encounter with a rhino — was receiving a lecture from a tall, khaki-clad man on the dangers of going into the bush alone!

PAST BETRAYALS
Giulia Gray

As soon as Jon realized that Julia had fallen in love with him, he broke off their relationship and returned to work in the Middle East. When Jon's best friend, Danny, proposed a marriage of friendship, Julia accepted. Then Jon returned and Julia discovered her love for him remained unchanged.

PRETTY MAIDS ALL IN A ROW
Rose Meadows

The six beautiful daughters of George III of England dreamt of handsome princes coming to claim them, but the King always found some excuse to reject proposals of marriage. This is the story of what befell the Princesses as they began to seek lovers at their father's court, leaving behind rumours of secret marriages and illegitimate children.

THE GOLDEN GIRL
Paula Lindsay

Sarah had everything — wealth, social background, great beauty and magnetic charm. Her heart was ruled by love and compassion for the less fortunate in life. Yet, when one man's happiness was at stake, she failed him — and herself.

A DREAM OF HER OWN
Barbara Best

A stranger gently kisses Sarah Danbury at her Betrothal Ball. Little does she realise that she is to meet this mysterious man again in very different circumstances.

HOSTAGE OF LOVE
Nara Lake

From the moment pretty Emma Tregear, the only child of a Van Diemen's Land magnate, met Philip Despard, she was desperately in love. Unfortunately, handsome Philip was a convict on parole.

THE ROAD TO BENDOUR
Joyce Eaglestone

Mary Mackenzie had lived a sheltered life on the family farm in Scotland. When she took a job in the city she was soon in a romantic maze from which only she could find the way out.

NEW BEGINNINGS
Ann Jennings

On the plane to his new job in a hospital in Turkey, Felix asked Harriet to put their engagement on hold, as Philippe Krir, the Director of Bodrum hospital, refused to hire 'attached' people. But, without an engagement ring, what possible excuse did Harriet have for holding Philippe at bay?

THE CAPTAIN'S LADY
Rachelle Edwards

1820: When Lianne Vernon becomes governess at Elswick Manor, she finds her young pupil is given to strange imaginings and that her employer, Captain Gideon Lang, is the most enigmatic man she has ever encountered. Soon Lianne begins to fear for her pupil's safety.

THE VAUGHAN PRIDE
Margaret Miles

As the new owner of Southwood Manor, Laura Vaughan discovers that she's even more poverty stricken than before. She also finds that her neighbour, the handsome Marius Kerr, is a little too close for comfort.

HONEY-POT
Mira Stables

Lovely, well-born, well-dowered, Russet Ingram drew all men to her. Yet here she was, a prisoner of the one man immune to her graces — accused of frivolously tampering with his young ward's romance!

DREAM OF LOVE
Helen McCabe

When there is a break-in at the art gallery she runs, Jade can't believe that Corin Bossinney is a trickster, or that she'd fallen for the oldest trick in the book . . .

FOR LOVE OF OLIVER
Diney Delancey

When Oliver Scott buys her family home, Carly retains the stable block from which she runs her riding school. But she soon discovers Oliver is not an easy neighbour to have. Then Carly is presented with a new challenge, one she must face for love of Oliver.

THE SECRET OF MONKS' HOUSE
Rachelle Edwards

Soon after her arrival at Monks' House, Lilith had been told that it was haunted by a monk, and she had laughed. Of greater interest was their neighbour, the mysterious Fabian Delamaye. Was he truly as debauched as rumour told, and what was the truth about his wife's death?